# SOMEWHERE A LONG AND HAPPY LIFE PROBABLY AWAITS YOU

# SOMEWHERE A LONG AND HAPPY LIFE PROBABLY AWAITS YOU

STORIES
**JILL SEXSMITH**

ARP Books  ·  Winnipeg

ARP Books (Arbeiter Ring Publishing)
201E-121 Osborne Street
Winnipeg, Manitoba
Canada R3L 1Y4
arpbooks.org

Cover image copyright © Julie Morstad
Book design and layout by Urban Ink, Winnipeg.
Printed and bound in Canada by Friesens on paper made from 100% recycled
post-consumer waste.

Conseil des Arts  Canada Council
du Canada      for the Arts

MANITOBA ARTS COUNCIL
CONSEIL DES ARTS DU MANITOBA

Canada      Manitoba

ARP Books acknowledges the generous support of the Manitoba Arts Council and the
Canada Council for the Arts for our publishing program. We acknowledge the financial
support of the Government of Canada through the Canada Book Fund and the Province
of Manitoba through the Book Publishing Tax Credit and the Book Publisher Marketing
Assistance Program of Manitoba Culture, Heritage, and Tourism.

Library and Archives Canada Cataloguing in Publication

Sexsmith, Jill, author

    Somewhere a long and happy life probably awaits you : stories / Jill Sexsmith.

Short stories.

ISBN 978-1-894037-71-6 (paperback)

    I. Title.

PS8637.E94S64 2016    C813'.6    C2016-900638-7

FOR MIKHAIL

# CONTENTS

# SOMEWHERE A LONG AND HAPPY LIFE PROBABLY AWAITS YOU

Manfred's wife, Elizabeth, pets the elm tree in their front yard. Last month, city workers painted a giant X on its trunk.

"Poor tree. It knows what orange spray paint means." Elizabeth flips open her phone and calls the city. "When will you be euthanizing my elm?"

Hedwig, their Polish neighbour, sits on her porch sipping pickle juice from a martini glass. "Don't be nostalgia," she yells. "I'm ready for change." She taps her oversized sun visor and points to the bald spot on her lawn where her tree used to stand.

"I hate to admit she has a point," Manfred says. "It is just a tree."

Manfred looks at the elm. He likes the tree as much as one can possibly like a tree, though he has always thought it was too close to the house and worried it might crash through the roof in a storm. He also hates all the raking in autumn and the way the sap shellacs the windows and makes bugs stick to it. He thinks some shrubs would be nice and doesn't exactly mind the idea of driving home one day to find a pile of sawdust.

"Sometime between May and September is not a date," Elizabeth shouts into her phone, then snaps it shut. "Why can't they just tell me when?"

"They work for the city. They can't commit."

She resumes petting the elm and offers to bring it tea. "You'll feel so much better."

Manfred would feel better if they were in the backyard, doing all of this tree comforting behind a fence. Lately, she wants to make everyone and everything a cup of Earl Grey. All of their houseplants are dying. The goldfish is already dead; Elizabeth flushed it, along with a tea bag.

"Why can't you see it's worth trying to save her?" Elizabeth leans against the tree. Shadows from the leaves make strange shapes dance across her face.

"Because we can just plant a new one. I've always liked boxwoods and we'd be less likely to wake up with them lying across our bed."

Manfred goes inside. Elizabeth will come in only when she is certain no chainsaw-wielding arborist from the city is going to charge down the street, strapped into one of those giant buckets.

Since the tree got sick, Manfred does like knowing where his wife will be: camped under the elm, hugging the elm. Throughout their marriage, Elizabeth has been known to wander.

*Safaris.*

This is what she calls it when she disappears. She either returns on her own, or Manfred gets a phone call and has to pick her up at the local Gymboree or the paintball field where she has been picketing. *Make love not war.*

At first, her safaris filled Manfred with a sense of urgency. His wife was missing! Later, she would be found in her underwear in a wading pool two blocks away. Sometimes he would try to wait it out; sometimes he would plaster the neighbourhood with missing posters.

"That tabby cat of yours lost again?" Hedwig would ask as he stapled a picture of Elizabeth's face to her tree.

The police rarely helped, because Elizabeth always left a note.

*On safari! Back in a jiffy.*

Once, when she didn't come back in a jiffy, Manfred became a suspect. He rode around in a police cruiser until they found her outside a community centre, running through sprinklers in the moonlight.

"Sorry, man," the officer said when he dropped them off at home. "That's got to suck."

"You have no idea."

When Elizabeth got out of the car, she was still soaking wet and left an outline of herself on the seat. She stood there on the curb, dripping. By then she was cold, the edges of her lips turning blue. Neighbours parted their curtains. When he got out of the car, Manfred wrapped a towel around her, which she removed and made into a turban.

"We lose ninety percent of our heat through our heads," she said.

Manfred gently guided her back inside the house and began to wonder what it would be like to be married to someone else.

From the nightstand, Elizabeth grabs her elephant bong, gets it smouldering with an expert flick of her lighter. By the glow of the flame, her self-inflicted haircut doesn't look as bad.

"It's the shattered look," she said when she came out of the bathroom with fistfuls of hair.

"It's really working," Manfred replied. He didn't know hair could look like that.

She inhales deeply, leans back and holds her breath until she sputters smoke.

"Want a hoot?"

Manfred nods and they pass the elephant between them.

When her doctor wouldn't give Elizabeth a marijuana prescription, she went straight to the pot store, grabbed the bong and said, "I've always wanted to smoke out of a trunk."

The clerk nodded and told her where she could score her first quarter.

When Elizabeth finally stops talking about Dutch elm disease and falls asleep, Manfred watches her eyeballs flutter beneath her lids. He is happy sleep comes easily tonight. Last week at her doctor's appointment, she complained of insomnia, how she bought things when she couldn't sleep: a leopard print Snuggie and the Slap Chop. She brought these to the appointment and laid them on the examination table.

Manfred wanted the doctor to give her drugs. It was a very simple solution provided by doctors everywhere all the time. But the doctor said, "You should enjoy life while you can."

Manfred realizes now that he should have come to his wife's rescue. But at that moment, all he could think about was ordering a new spouse off a late-night infomercial—one with parts in working order and under warranty, one more convenient, one who didn't need to be implanted with a GPS tracking device. All he could think about was getting some sleep. He couldn't stand another night of hearing about four easy payments.

"Some barbiturates, please," he said.

He tries not to think of that now, of the way he acted or did not act. He pulls a blanket up to Elizabeth's chin, bends down and feels her exhale gently in his ear. The smell of her breath always reminds him of sweet corn. He hovers above her and nibbles the air, tries to think of her good qualities.

Manfred met Elizabeth when she interviewed for a position at his fortune cookie company. She was a greeting card writer looking to branch out.

"I thought you'd be Asian," she said when she sat down. Her hair was a tangle and she had a few disposable chopsticks stuck in it.

"I'm Swedish," he said, trying to sound offended.

After a long pause, she pulled out her portfolio of get well soon, sympathy and wedding cards.

*You're sick. That sucks. © Elizabeth*

*I'm sooooo sorry. © Elizabeth*

*Ah, wedding bells. Ring-a-ding-ding. © Elizabeth*

"Why do you want the position?" Manfred asked as he leafed through her work.

"I like short sentences."

"Sounds reasonable."

"So, you're not even a little bit Asian?" she asked. "I wore these chopsticks to make a good impression." She pointed to the ones impaling her bun.

"Nope, still Swedish."

She wanted to see how fortune cookies were made, so he toured her around the plant until she wandered off and got lost among the twirling vats. He realizes now he should have taken this as a sign. But there was a certain excitement in following her, in finding her. He rarely came onto the factory floor. She made everything he did seem interesting.

That day, when Manfred found her again, she was holding a handful of broken cookies and had a stack of fortunes pinched between her fingers.

"These are very pedestrian," she said. "Trust me. You need me."

Manfred wakes in the morning and Elizabeth is gone. He fights that familiar feeling of relief and dread. Before he looks for her, he thinks about lying diagonally in the bed, maybe splaying out like a starfish. He lifts the covers and looks at the line Elizabeth duct-tapes down the middle every time they change the sheets.

She said, "Even people who live together need to be invited to the other side."

Manfred liked this idea. Even when she was on safari, he didn't cross it. Now he stretches his foot over to her side, very slowly. The fabric is cold against his foot and calf. He lets only his big toe touch the edge before he pulls it back to his side.

When Manfred goes out to the front yard, Elizabeth is holding a one-woman protest. She bobs her sign up and down—*Save the Elm!*—and marches around the tree, occasionally switching directions to unwind. Neighbours walk by and nod or smile or grip their children's hands a little tighter. Elizabeth has made them *that* couple.

"I've called an arborist," Elizabeth says. "I want a second opinion." She has dark circles under her eyes. A dozen cankerworms have dropped from the tree and are humping their way across the top of her head.

Manfred waits with her. When the arborist pulls up and gets out of his truck, Elizabeth says, "This guy better have excellent tree-side manners." She offers him tea, but he shakes his head.

"She's a beauty, isn't she?" The arborist touches the bark and gently peels back a few layers like they are gauze bandages. "These are feeding galleries." He points to marks on the tree that look like woodcarvings in the shape of starbursts.

"Can it be cured?" Elizabeth asks.

"I'd bet my left nut it's too late for this one." He tells her treatments will prolong life, not cure anything. "These things rot from the inside out. Before you know it, they're hollow."

Elizabeth pets the elm. "You're sick. That sucks."

"Do you want to go ahead with treatments?" the arborist asks.

Elizabeth nods. He grabs a giant needle from his kit. She looks away while he injects deep into the trunk.

"Enjoy her while she's still standing." The arborist leaves.

Elizabeth turns to Manfred, clings to her sign. "I wish we had built our house around the tree. You see that sometimes, a tree in the living room. I might have noticed it getting sick."

Even though she is right in front of Manfred, she looks like a missing person.


Inside, Elizabeth starts putting on her work clothes. Manfred asks if she'd like to stay home instead. She is down to one day a week anyway and naps under her desk for most of it.

"I need to be productive. People depend on me to tell them how their futures will turn out."

He wants her to stay home and rest, but mostly he needs her to stay home because she is terrible for business. Her fortunes have become increasingly pessimistic and suppliers are complaining.

*A dark shadow moves with you.*

*The time for romance has passed.*

*Somewhere a long and happy life probably awaits you.*

This is not the kind of news people want to get after eating their ginger beef noodles and wonton soup. But Elizabeth confessed it makes her feel better to make other people worry. Just a little.

"Don't you want to relax and read some books? We can stop paying Hedwig to watch the elm. I really hate how she stuffs my money into her bra."

"She needs the money. Besides, a pile of books will just remind me of all the stories I'll never get to."

"We all have stories we won't get to." This strikes Manfred as the wrong thing to say. He wonders if he will do better with his next wife.

Elizabeth lies down and agrees to stay home. She asks Manfred to install a baby monitor by the elm so she will be able to hear chainsaws if they come while she is sleeping.

"They can't just sneak up on me like that," Elizabeth says. "I need fair warning."

Manfred buys and installs the monitor. "Anything else?" He holds his wife's hand.

Elizabeth puts the monitor to her ear. "I would really love a tree house."


On his way to work, Manfred mentally sketches in more of his new wife: Samantha. She likes the same radio stations he does. There is no zipping back and forth between the oldies and New Age flutes. She likes to travel and, unlike Elizabeth, does not need to wear a harness and leash in a crowd.

Samantha is kind. She has never had career ambitions. To pass time, she volunteers at an animal rescue shelter and specializes in the care of lop-eared bunnies previously used for research. When she is not caring directly for the animals, she canvases local grocery stores for donations of lettuce and carrots. Manfred likes Samantha's legs. Even in her Humane Society uniform, he can tell they are sexy.

Samantha has a small scar below her left knee. She got it when she was twelve, during her professional skateboarder phase, which, incidentally, only lasted one day. The injury knocked her out of her chosen career.

Samantha comes from a normal family. When her mother (Eleanor/ please call me Mom) carves the turkey at Christmas, she does not talk about her mastectomy as she slices off the bird's breast. As the meat falls into a neat pile, she does not talk about skin biopsies. Eleanor does not wear low-cut tops that show a swoosh of scar tissue, still howling years later. In Samantha's family, they don't even eat meat.

At the factory, Manfred goes into Elizabeth's office. He looks at the fort under her desk where she often works by flashlight. He slowly removes the unfinished fortunes tacked to a corkboard.

*You will never be...*

*You will not have...*

*You will not meet...*

Manfred puts them in an envelope. He looks at the other things in her fort: a blanket, pillows, slippers. She even has a curtain for complete darkness. Manfred crawls under and pulls it shut. Glow-in-the-dark constellations and a sliver of moon light up the underside of her desk. She has her own universe here.

Manfred stays under the desk until he feels it's a respectable time for a boss to leave. When he pulls into the driveway, he finds Elizabeth—in her wedding dress—picking a bouquet of flowers from Hedwig's garden.

"Let's renew our vows," she says.

"No need." Manfred has an acute awareness of the neighbour's curtains parting. "Let's get you inside."

Elizabeth sits down with a daisy and starts pulling off the petals. "He loves me. He loves me not. He loves me."

"You can't keep doing things like this."

"He loves me not, not, not, not, not." She throws the bouquet over her shoulder. The petals flail, then scatter on the ground.

Hedwig comes out in her robe. She touches Elizabeth on the shoulder and guides her toward a different patch of daisies. Quietly, to Manfred, Hedwig says, "In case you didn't know, shit dip, your wife is dying."

When Elizabeth has revived her bouquet, she walks toward Manfred, holding up her dress with her free hand. He is struck by all of the fabric around her—so much empty space between her and the dress. When they first got married, there was so much of her. She bulged and occupied space. Her breasts spilled out of the gown like she had a spare set.

Manfred collects her and carries her inside. He remembers how *she* carried *him* over the threshold on their wedding night. As he lays her down on the bed, she feels like a pile of bones. Her bouquet falls apart on her chest.

Manfred grabs Elizabeth's hand and says, "I do."

She quietly recites her old vows. "I promise to make you falafels from scratch every fourth Saturday morning. I will never leave the cap off the toothpaste or my towel in the sink. I will have an adventure every day and always invite you."

When it opens the next morning, Manfred goes straight to Home Depot.

It seems many people go to Home Depot on Saturday mornings. Manfred has never been. He has never been keen to fix things.

He wanders up and down the aisles. An older man wearing an apron asks Manfred if he has found all he is looking for. Manfred asks where he can find two-by-fours and rustproof nails. The man shows him. Manfred can tell he likes his job but hates his apron. He tries to make it look manlier by sticking a tape measure and a utility knife in its pouches.

Manfred shows him the tree house manual. The man tells him which coloured lines on the floor he needs to follow. Manfred rolls along and the things he needs pile up in his cart.

When Manfred gets home, city workers are re-marking Elizabeth's tree. Hedwig is there, arguing with them. Finally, she spits and pulls a wad of money from her bra. The workers leave, counting the loot between them.

Hedwig says, "You have until the end of September, shit dip. Don't blow it."

He sees she has turned off the baby monitor. When he gets inside, Elizabeth is asleep, still in her filthy wedding dress.

While Manfred takes his supplies out of the car, Hedwig sends over her son, Bolesław.

"I quit college and am boring. Can I help?"

With no previous tree house-making skills, Manfred accepts. Hedwig sits down in her chair, swings her leg over an armrest and says, "I'm foreman."

Together, Bolesław and Manfred make a rope ladder and swing it over the tree. Manfred climbs up. They make a hoist and Bolesław sends planks up, late into the evening. From the ground, Hedwig shouts instructions that surprisingly make sense. When they are done making a semi-level platform, Manfred holds the hammer over his head.

When Elizabeth wakes, she wanders outside looking disoriented, complaining she is cold. "Have you seen my roach clip?" she calls out to a woman walking her Yorkie.

"Look," Manfred says, "for you." He is standing in the tree, feeling a bit like Tarzan.

Bolesław helps Elizabeth up the ladder. She sits in her new home and pets the tree's upper limbs. "All better," she says. "All better."

Even as a child, Manfred never wanted a tree house. Now that he is in one, he sees the appeal and wishes they had done this long ago. He holds a fallen leaf to Elizabeth's face. "Green is your colour."

The next day, Manfred and Bolesław build four straight-ish walls while Elizabeth sits on the front steps and writes slightly more optimistic fortunes.

*Something of value may be returned this week.*

*Almost everything you do, you do with grace.*

When they're done, they move some things into the tree, including Elizabeth's chaise—a beautiful piece of furniture that never gets used. Bolesław makes her a dumbwaiter out of a cooler and a rope. He tells her he will make her tea any time. "Day and night. Just ring my bell."

Elizabeth sits down, folds up her fortunes like little airplanes and dive-bombs everyone who walks by.

"It's your almost-lucky day," she says when they look up.

Throughout the summer, Elizabeth and Manfred slowly move into the tree house. They plant impatiens and put them in the windowsill. They watch them grow. They string up white lights and turn them on every evening. At night, they press close on the chaise to keep each other warm. There is no duct tape.

Manfred starts working from their tree home. Cellphone reception is great. They take in a pet squirrel. They make the community newspaper: *Lovebirds Nest in Dying Elm.*

When their neighbours walk by, Elizabeth waves them up the ladder. They never had company in their house—the one below with the broken windows and a small forest growing in the eaves. But here the people come, climbing up a rope ladder to sit in their tree house.

Elizabeth smokes less pot and seems to get high off the neighbourhood gossip: Richard and Carol are both having an affair with their cleaning lady; the Watsons got a fine for not mowing their lawn; the Tanners' daughter ran away a few weeks ago (they think she is a drug addict and prostitute); Mr. Fergus is going blind but insists it makes him a better driver.

When Elizabeth has had enough, she writes each guest a special fortune and sends them on their way.

*Nothing wrong with sharing.*

*Long grass is underrated.*

*Your child wants to be found.*


As autumn approaches, the days grow shorter. The leaves change colour and the peach of Elizabeth's face drains along with them. The air holds a faint smell of decay and there is something damp and rotting about her scent too. At night, Manfred does his best to ignore the elm bark beetles that burrow into his pyjamas and hair.

"These are the last stages," the arborist tells them as he sinks in the final needle. "We should stop treatment now."

Elizabeth seems ready.

Some nights, Manfred can't ignore the beetles. He flicks them off, but they multiply. "I have to go in. Please come with me."

Elizabeth shakes her head. "I have to get used to this. I don't want to be cremated."

By the faint light of the street lamp, he watches beetles crawl across her face. "I wish I had gone on more safaris with you."

In the beginning she did invite him and he went, following her through a farmer's field to pet a newborn goat, driving her far away from the city lights so they could see a comet that wouldn't be visible again in their lifetime. He thought they were making "remember when" moments, doing things they could look back on when their lives had become so normal they were unrecognizable. But Elizabeth had no intention of stopping. She went on and would go on without him.

When Manfred does make it through the night outside, they wake covered in a blanket of leaves. He brushes them off. Elizabeth sweeps them away, then sits on the floor looking up, terrified of the next one to fall. When she is not sweeping, she sleeps or reads a few sentences, then puts her book down.

"I guess my brain is as full as it's going to get. I'll never know the history of the British Empire and I'm never going to finish *Ulysses*."

"No one finishes *Ulysses* and if they say they have they're lying."

She says she is cold. He rolls her up in a duvet.

"I want to be closer to the sun," she says.

It is approaching late September. Manfred looks at the tree and thinks there is still time to build a second storey.

When Manfred returns to Home Depot, his friend in the apron is not there to guide him. There are no people in the aisles. He buys more cedar boards and a manual on how to build a staircase. He looks at it and hopes Hedwig will loan him Bolesław again.

On the way back, before Manfred is on his street, he hears the angry buzz of a chainsaw. He drives up to find Elizabeth chewing away at the tree while city workers smoke cigarettes and guide her. The saw eats into the trunk, then kicks back. She keeps gouging.

"Whack, whack," she yells as Manfred approaches. She holds the saw above her head.

She takes a few more runs at the tree until the saw gets stuck and Manfred pulls her away. For a small woman, she has done a lot of damage. All around the base of the tree, there are big chunks missing. The elm groans, then leans slightly.

"I decide when it's over," she says.

Manfred tells her about the supplies strapped to the roof of their car. "There's still time."

Leaves swirl at their feet. The tree cracks again.

"Timber!" Hedwig yells.

They move out of the way and watch the tree rush toward the pavement and a row of parked cars. The crash shakes the neighbourhood, breaks glass, crushes metal, sets off alarms.

Manfred hears Elizabeth exhale, then feels her hand slip away. A small crowd gathers around the tree. Among the people and broken limbs, he loses sight of her.

"Such a shame nothing could be done," they say. "She really added character to the neighbourhood."

Manfred does not look for her this time. He just stands there. His car is untouched, the lumber and supplies still strapped to the roof. He keeps looking at it until the light fades and all he can see is an outline of a staircase he will never build.

# THIS IS AN EPIC LOVE STORY

She watches the red truck approach for miles—a tiny flame on the horizon. As it gets closer, it picks up speed. A dog with a sloppy tongue sticks its head out the passenger window. She swears it mocks her as the truck passes, disappearing into its own cloud.

When everything settles, the truck is stopped in the distance. The brake lights flash on and off. The driver reverses.

"Strange to see someone so far out here," the driver yells out his window. Then he kicks the passenger door open. "You almost blend into the desert."

She has pulled her shirt over her head for protection from the sun. If her face looks anything like her arms, it is chapped and crusted with sand. She drags herself into the truck.

"Time for a shower," the driver says, but he does not really look at her and for this she is grateful. He hits the accelerator and the door swings shut. His hair is drawn back into a loose ponytail. The skin on his neck and forearms looks caramelized. Edible.

His three-legged dog growls at her. She has taken its spot.

"Can you give me water?"

Before he answers, she reaches for his thermos and guzzles warm coffee. When she spits it out, the dog bares teeth, then clamps down on her arm.

The driver stops, hauls the dog into the back, rips the sleeve off his shirt and wraps her bleeding wrist. His hands feel like cat's tongue against her blistered skin. He knots the fabric with a jerk. She wants to cry but it seems like a waste of water. In the visor mirror, she can only see her lips, filled with cracks deep enough to fall into. She hangs her head and feels pulled over by the weight of it.

He digs around in his cooler and puts an ice cube in her mouth. She rests her head against the seat.

"Fire," she says.

"You're in a rough way." His voice softens and she feels him really look at her.

"I'm fucking dying."


At the hospital, the machine beside her makes a reassuring beep. She is its echo.

"Beep. Beep. Beep."

The doctor smiles a concerned-yet-slightly-amused-by-you smile then slides a thermometer into her mouth.

"How long were you wandering in the desert?"

"A few years."

"Were you alone?"

"An old man gave me a ride. There were some chickens and a lizard, the kind that walk on two legs and have a frill around the neck. He wanted sunscreen."

The doctor nods and checks her blood pressure.

"It was so quiet I could hear the lizard blink."

Fluid from a bag drips into her forearm. The doctor lifts the bandage on her elbow.

"Did the lizard bite you?"

"No, he stole my map."

The doctor presses a cold pack to her forehead.

"Is there anyone we can call for you?"

"The lizard's name is Marty but he didn't give me his phone number. Bastard."

"Things will be better the next time you wake up."

In her dark hospital room, sounds from a game show leak under her door. A contestant shrieks, overwhelmed by the possibility of a stackable washer and dryer. In bed, she moves from side to side, watches the IV drip.

Sand blows under the door and she feels her sheet blow around her in the warm desert wind. She hears the nurses talk about Christmas. It can't be celebrated in the desert. In the morning, she'll have to let them know.

A doctor is paged. The door opens. Someone slips a straw between her lips. She wants to flood herself, store up. She thinks about the convenience of becoming a camel. She smells urine but cannot tell if it is hers. She fears she has been diapered.

"Temporarily." The nurse brushes hair off her patient's forehead.

"Have you seen my chicken?"

The nurse shakes her head and smiles.

She feels something small and round on the tip of her tongue.

"Swallow."

"My chicken answers to Diablo and he's leash trained. His wing may or may not be in a sling. Otherwise, I'm afraid he looks like an ordinary chicken."

She opens her eyes and he slowly comes into focus. He sits by the window, still wearing his shirt with one sleeve.

"How are you feeling?"

"Melted."

"What's your name?"

"Crayola."

"Do you remember anything about how you got here?"

"I rode into town on a three-headed dog."

The next time she wakes, he is beside her.

"Do you want me to put my dog down?"

"The one with three heads?" She looks at the bandage on her arm, peels the corner up and looks under it.

"Yeah, that one. Only it's three legs, not heads."

"I suppose he's already been through enough. Can you put me down?"

"Can I bring you anything?"

"Was I carrying a bag when you found me?"

He shakes his head.

"Then you can bring me everything."

The nurse wheels her into a room where a cool bath has been prepared. Tiny geckos tile the walls and scatter out the window as the door opens. The nurse rolls over a straggler. The gecko wiggles, then scurries away, leaving its tail behind.

She winces.

"Their tails grow back." The nurse pats her shoulder and helps her stand. "Can you manage on your own?"

"I swam the English Channel when I was five. I should be fine."

"Pull the string if you need me."

She undresses and licks her salty skin. As she moves, she feels as if she doesn't have enough skin to go around her, as if she lost some out there. Is this something you go looking for? Missing skin.

Her hair is fried too. The ends snap off in her hands. She scatters them in the tub and thinks about feeding ducks. She enters the water. Clay, dried to her body, makes a red plume. Through the mirror on the wall, she sees lines of sanguine run down her face and cut it into sections. Cheeks. Lips. Eyes. Nose. This country wants her in pieces.

The gecko with no tail sits at the edge of the tub.

"Does it hurt?" she asks.

"Nope. It's just embarrassing."

"Do you know Marty?"

The gecko nods and licks his eyelids.

"If you see him, tell him I want my map back."

He brings her everything. She holds up a new T-shirt and sees he has gone shopping for her in the children's department.

"Why do you keep coming here?"

"You're the most interesting thing that's ever landed in the desert."

At night, in her room, sand continues to blow under the door. She gets up and walks across the desert. She walks past a branch, soon covered. A skull with a buried jaw. There is always something trying to grow. And failing. Though there are variations in colour, she can describe it only as empty.

She looks for a tumbleweed. All this time out here and not one bloody tumbleweed or cactus. She feels lied to. Will file a complaint.

The red dunes form a crest. She walks along it—the spine of a beast. Sleepy. Lumbering. Vertebrae are crushed under the weight of her heels. In the moonlight, a dead tree walks toward her. She will tell it her story. It will give her an impartial ruling.

There is complete silence. Strangely heavy. She clucks her tongue and snaps her fingers—so dry she sees a spark. An engine hums in the distance. A grey truck circles back. She looks for a cactus to hide behind. Still nothing.

"Just stand still and I'll hit the chicken, not you."

The old man adjusts his glasses as they slide down his sweaty nose. Slippery finger on a trigger. She thinks about his breath. How she expected ashtray and cheap whiskey but got fresh liquorice instead, maybe a hint of

Gummi bear. He was so close she thought he would lick or kiss her—the threat of it almost worse than the act.

"Just a few more seconds while I get my aim straight."

The chicken grows restless, knows her head is not a proper roost. There is a shot. A bullet clips a wing. At first she cannot tell who is bleeding. A squawking truck full of poultry goes silent. She hangs onto the chicken, tries wrapping its wing, but it gets away and goes flapping over the dune.

"Have a nice life," the old man says and gets back in his truck. "I just shot your dinner."

When the truck is a speck, she goes looking for the chicken and finds it on its side, spinning in circles. She wishes she were brave enough to snap its neck. Instead, she wraps its wing and tucks it under her arm. Eventually, it stops moving.

Marty drops by to see how she is doing.

"Not so good."

When the sun starts to come up, the tree in the distance is still. Its arms hang by its side. Limp and unsure.


The doctor presses her arm and removes the IV. The long needle leaves the vein, more pressure, the sting of alcohol, a new bandage. She looks at the holes they have poked in her arm.

"All set?" he asks.

"I prefer Superman Band-Aids."

The doctor gives her one last concerned-for-you smile and pats her back. He helps her out of bed.

"I'm allergic to latex." She picks at her Band-Aid. Does not want to go outside before she feels ready.

The nurse walks her to the door.

Outside, the sky is blue, the sun raw and pulsing. She shields her eyes and looks for a shadow. Feels like she will spend the rest of her life looking for shade.

He leans against his truck while the dog sleeps underneath. Sun shines through pieces of rusted metal. Behind him, ribbons of red sand stretch on forever.

"We're the last people on earth," she says.

"We just might be."

He helps her into the truck, puts a small pot of salve on the seat between them.

"For your lips." He points to his lips.

She rubs it on and feels a cool tingle spread across her mouth.

As they drive, he asks, "Can you remember anything more about how you got to the desert?"

"I got a ride with a chicken farmer. He made room for me in the back of his truck."

"And then?"

"I stared at squawking chickens piled on top of each other. One shit on my head. He felt really bad about it."

"Anything else?"

She hooks her thumbs in her armpits and flaps. "They didn't know the chicken dance. You'd think it would come naturally. But, no."

He pulls up to a doorway carved into the side of a hill. He opens it and leads her down a gently sloped hallway that spirals deep underground. She touches the walls and shelves cut out of sandstone. There are red stains on her hands.

"What is this?"

"Abandoned opal mine. Lots of people here live in them."

While she was in the hospital, he carved out a spare bedroom. The three-legged dog hops behind them. She wants to stay away from it but offers her hand instead. He licks it.

"He's marinating me."

"He likes you."

"Does he have a name?"

"Doesn't need one."

"I've heard you call him Get-Over-Here, Stay and Come. Choose one."

"Come."

He sits on the edge of her bed as she unpacks everything. More shirts. A sunhat with a chinstrap and whistle. Pants with an elastic waistband. She pulls out a box of tampons and thinks she might fall in love.


At night, when she can't sleep, he comes and sits on a chair beside her bed.

"What can you tell me about the lizard?"

"He was very lizardy."

"You called him Marty?"

She nods.

"Can you tell me anything else about him?"

"He carried a briefcase."

"What do you think that means?"

"He was a business lizard."

"Where did he come from?"

"I opened my eyes and there he was. He said he was part of neighbourhood watch and clearly I was a damsel in distress."

"Anything else?"

"He gave me directions to the highway. When he walked away, his footprints disappeared faster than he could lay them down."

"How did that make you feel?"

"Like he was never there."


In the morning, she tries on one of the children's shirts. It rips around the neck, pulls deep into her armpits; the word *princess* stretches across her chest.

"You want to borrow one of mine?"

She pulls off the one he is wearing. He fumbles with the training bra he bought her—a thick band of elastic with no hooks. There is sand in her sheets and they grind it into each other's skin. Come lies on the floor, occasionally lifting his head and whimpering.

"Stay with me, at least until you feel well enough to travel."

She feels a grain of sand fall into her ear.

On the way to his mining claim, the truck rocks back and forth over the dunes. As they crest each one, there is more of the same—sand with lines carved out by wind and things that slither, patches of scrub, signs that warn of unmarked holes.

"Can you tell me anything about where you come from?"

"I'm the daughter of a diplomat. I went to school in the Emirates and Switzerland. I can downhill ski, play chess, speak French, Italian and Arabic. I know which fork to use at a formal dinner. I'm an accomplished equestrian. My first pony was named Boutros Boutros-Ghali."

"Really?"

"No."

When they get out of the truck, he guides her toward a dark hole. At the edge, she steps into a harness, his thick fingers fumble with the buckles.

"You've never successfully unhooked a woman's bra have you?"

"No."

She tugs on the cable, not convinced it's attached to anything. He offers to go down first. She considers this a good sign but knows if she doesn't go now, she never will. Her boot touches the first metal rung, then she lowers the rest of her body down and feels swallowed whole.

"You'll get used to going down," he yells.

She hears the clack-clack sound of the winch as it spools out more cable. She moves down and her ankle gets wrapped in the safety rope. She shakes it free and keeps searching for the next rung. A breeze from within hits her skin—soft, like an exhale. When she touches down, she undoes the harness, feels along the folds of the mine, moist and rippled. In the darkness, she waits.

She listens to him make his way down, sure-footed. She can tell he does not pause to think about slipping or broken bones or needing rescue. The sound of his breath presses against her. She is startled by his hands as they find her in the dark. He tells her to wait while he lights a candle.

Soon, the widest part of the mine glows. Deep tunnels branch off in every direction. The walls are opalescent creams, bleeding into reds and green. She runs her hand over it, rough like an oyster shell.

"Is this opal?" She looks at the small scratches on her palm.

He shakes his head. "Potch. It's worthless."

On the ground, arranged on a blanket, there is a bottle of whiskey, two shot glasses, a bag of baby carrots, a loaf of white bread and a package of bologna.

"A picnic," he says.

His mouth moves across her eyelids; his shirt goes over her head. She presses his back against the cold floor, grabs a handful of red earth and says, "Mark me."

With his index finger, he writes, *I was here.*

At the end of the night, their candle dies down. An empty whiskey bottle rolls away and smashes.


In bed, he inspects a tiny piece of opal held by tweezers. Then he presses the stone to her finger.

"What is opal made of?"

"Cooled lava and steam. What are you made of?"

"Sand."

"I need you to tell me one real thing about you."

"My favourite colour is periwinkle."

"Tell me more about the old man in the desert." He puts down the opal.

"He had flies all over him, pooling at the corners of his eyes, crawling in and out of his ears and nose, playing in his hair. He was a jungle gym for flies."

"Anything else?"

"He was very disrespectful to chickens."

"Can you describe him?"

"Impossibly ugly."

He leaves for work and she stays in the rabbit hole. She listens to the truck pull away and rolls the opal between her fingers before she puts it in her mouth, then spits it out.

Even from a distance, she feels tremors as miners punch new holes underground and blow them out with heavy machinery. What took him months to dig by hand, they will have in a few hours and if they get nothing, they move on.

"Opal waits millions of years to be found," he told her.

"That's a long time."

While he is underground, digging his claim with a thimble, she steps outside, lets the wind push her forward and leaves everything behind.

A new highway. A new driver. A new city. A new doctor. The same questions.

"Once he gave you the chicken what did he make you do?"

"Put it on my head."

"And then?"

"After the first shot, the chicken shit itself."

"What happened next?"

"I told him he had bad aim. Then I tried to find the chicken and fix its wing. It was a terrible patient. It was like it didn't want to be helped."

"I think you should stay here for a few days. Until we get this story straight."

"As long as there are thick curtains. I don't have a good relationship with the sun."

He fills in her room with red sand. Buries everything. He floods the old mine and starts a new claim. This time, he blows it wide open and deep. Uses gelignite to pulverize what lies beneath. He is anxious to get to the bottom of something. He sits in his truck, watches the desert convulse, then settle. Convulse, then settle. Come sits beside him and licks an imaginary paw.

She walks across the desert in bare feet, hand extended. A red truck stops. A door swings open.

The nurse comes in and tells her to get off the bed.

The earth is cracked and scorching. Her skin split.

The other patient in the room groans each time the mattress springs creak.

The sun is a strobe in her eyes. In flashes, he drives away without her.

"That's not how it happened," she says. "He comes back."

The nurse calls for help.

She sees Marty baking on a ledge.

Fingernails tap a syringe.

Startled, Marty flares the frill around his neck.

She feels the weight of a man on her back.

Marty opens his briefcase. "I heard you were miffed about this." He hands her the map.

She unfolds it. "Which way is back to him?"

Marty points his green finger and turns full circle. "I'm pretty sure it's that way."

She feels a dog bite. A bandage tighten around her arm. She feels the tingle of mint spread across her lips. She feels a dog lick her hand. The pull of a T-shirt over her head. The sound of fabric ripping.

She feels a grain of sand fall into her ear. The weight of it knocks her over.

# THE PROBLEM WITH BABIES

You watch for Ava through the crack in your office door. She is coming to work today to show off her newborn—something you both swore you would never do. You told her you refused to congratulate people for having sex without using birth control.

You have always thought of babies as being a bit like cancer—tumours with arms and legs. You have never understood why someone would willingly grow one.

Your favourite word is barren. Your motto: *save yourself.* When invited to a baby shower, you send a Diaper Genie and your regrets.

Recently though, you've been feeling a bit restless, gassy, empty. You ask your doctor what all the rumbling is about; wonder if it's *the urge* you hear other women talk about.

"Don't get too crazy," he says, "it could just be an irritable bowel."

He recommends you snack on fennel seeds and sip ginger tea. So you do. You snack. You sip. Things seem to settle down.

When Ava arrives, the newborn is cradled in her arms—a tiny wailing thing wrapped in a blanket covered with ducks. She takes it to the lounge for its installation. She is pretty much your last friend to become a mother and, as these things go, the latest friend you have lost or are about to lose. You get out of your chair. You want to get your *ooh ah* over and done with. You want to get on with your day.

Ava and her baby quickly draw a group of admirers. You hide behind them and assess everyone's sincerity, willingness to lie, desperation to get out of work. Faces are scrunched up, lips are puckered, there are genuine-sounding *oohs* and *ahs*, soft tickles on the baby's chin and cheeks.

"Awen't you pwecious."

You wonder what happens to Rs when a baby is present. An entire letter from the alphabet disappears.

Ava opens her diaper bag and the pristine lounge becomes a sprawling mess of gender-neutral toys and wet naps. You are used to an Ava carved by hard angles: tailored suits nipped in at her tiny waist, hair cut blunt with a razor, stilettos worn like weapons. This Ava is soft around the edges, wears no make-up. This Ava has short hair and wears a leisure suit.

As a few people leave, you move closer. This Ava seems tired but happy—*I am mother, hear me coo*. When she sees you, she smiles a weary smile. You almost expect her to apologize for procreating. For being a traitor.

"Cute?" she says and points to her baby.

You shrug. During labour, this baby came out swinging and separated Ava's pelvis. You can't help but feel hostile toward something that has assaulted your friend and will never be formally charged or serve time. This is the problem with babies: no matter what they've done, parents tend to be proud of them. In most cases, they have only burst out of the womb causing great bodily harm. But what were they going to do? Stay in there?

When your co-worker is done goochy gooing the baby, she passes it off to you like a football. You wonder if it would be bad to drop a baby. Likely, perhaps, absolutely. If you do, no matter what you achieve in your career, you will always be known simply as The Baby Dropper. So you hang onto the baby while it cries and digs its nails into your forearms. When it opens its mouth, it reveals its flailing tongue. It has a wrinkly face and looks like an old man stuffed into a baby's body. You make the baby do a little air dance thing. You think it should probably skip college and fill out the pension application right away.

"Wee," you say, setting it on the table—very gently—propped up by books on Cubism and the Renaissance.

The baby is scooped by someone else, which is when you notice its fingernails—impossibly tiny and delicate, attached to ten perfect little fingers.

"Do you have them manicured?" you ask.

Ava is busy wiping spittle and making a toy donkey bray, but a co-worker tells you she used to bite her daughter's nails while she slept. You reach for the baby's hand and feel compelled to nibble. You have never considered fingernails before—these tender morsels.

"Are they a standard feature on all babies?" you ask.

Without really knowing who she is talking to, Ava says, "Yessy wessy they are. Yes, they are. Yes, they are."

You return to your office where you chew on a few fennel seeds. You remember asking Ava how she decided she wanted to have a baby. She told you she was watching figure skating on TV. One had nothing to do with the other. Not really. Except that now, whenever she thinks of her child, she also thinks of triple Salchows and the one-foot Lutz.

"But how did you know it was what you wanted?" you asked.

"My TV was on the fritz. It paused while Midori Ito was mid-leap. And I just said, by the time she lands, I want to have made a big decision. So I chose baby."

"Just like that?"

"Figure skaters. They fling themselves in the air and hope for the best. I wanted to do the same."

You spend the next hour tracing the little half-moon indents the baby left on your arm. When they fade completely, you are sad, lonesome, relieved to see them go.

After work, you drive to Itsy Bitsy, a baby clothing boutique. You owe Ava a gift and you want to shake off this fingernail business.

The boutique is sandwiched between your favourite shoe store and café. Women with babies always come in, charging toward the espresso machine with their strollers, expecting people to move for them like they've got some sort of disability. Or they take up three times the space they need—parking strollers, baby seats and pop-up jumpy castles in the middle of the floor. The mothers look proud of their children as they entertain the crowd. You have always occupied one table, one chair. You pride yourself on being compact. You entertain no one.

Inside Itsy Bitsy, the store clerks hover around a stroller. A baby's designer booties kick the air. The mother beams at the child like it's her project, her exhibition, just a small sample from her successful breeding program. As you get closer, the baby is gnawing on a rubber set of keys. It, too, has the teensy fingernails.

You look for an outfit for Ava's baby. Mother Ava who said she never wanted a baby and can't even make two-sided photocopies. You sift through the racks. The clothes are overpriced, ridiculous, slowly winning you over. You grab an outfit and admire, mock, covet it.

"That's a onesie," the clerk says.

You figure onesies are part of the problem not part of the solution, but you say you'll take it and a few other things you've grabbed.

"When are you due?" The clerk starts rolling the onesie so it looks like a pansy.

You almost laugh then say, "May. Early May." You rub your stomach clockwise then counter.

"Congratulations," the clerk says, "wait right here."

She comes back holding a platter with a mini-Bundt cake on it. The top is shaped like a pregnant woman's stomach. She sticks a sparkler in the belly button and lights it. The hissing makes others gather around. They sing a congratulations jingle.

You sign up for Itsy Bitsy e-news. The Itsy Bitsy team is part of your family now, here to help you through this. You promise to let them know the very second you give birth. You start to think about the advantages of being pregnant: pre-boarding, the best parking spots, being congratulated for doing nothing, fucking, the miracle of life. When you are an expecting mother, no one cares that you can't tie your own shoes. They don't stop you on the street and ask to see your CV. People just want to rub your tummy, buy you things, feed you.

You stand with your Itsy Bitsy sisters until the sparkler blows itself out. Motherhood already makes you feel a bit guilty.

After work, you drive to your husband's office. He is still at work because he is too kind to say no to a patient mourning the death of one of seventeen cats. On the way to his office, you caress the baby clothes—a ruffled skirt, a sailor dress, frilly underwear. Pink mittens. The teensiest mittens, likely knitted by an elf. You want to frame these mittens. You suppose unisex clothes would have been more practical but if you were going to have a baby, she would have to be a girl. She'd have no choice. You refuse to bake a penis. For a moment, you forget these clothes are supposed to be a gift for your friend.

At Eric's office, you walk in and say, "Our baby-making sex will be the best we've ever had."

"This is sudden." He taps his desk with a pencil, looks worried, amused, bored.

"Sometimes it works this way."

"Since this morning when I saw you take your birth control?"

"Things change in a split second. Between this morning and that moment, there were ten thousand seconds and that many opportunities to change."

"Do you remember when you demanded we get exchange students so you could practice your Mandarin? Or when you wanted to install a salt-water fish tank so you could quit your job and breed seahorses?"

You finger an Itsy Bitsy soother in the bottom of your purse and want to shove it in his mouth. Of course you remember these things. "All wonderful ideas," you say.

His assistant pages him. His next patient is here.

"Mrs. Jamison?" you ask. "Is she the one who pulls out her eyelashes?"

He nods. "You can't return a baby by the way. Even if you keep the receipt." He kisses your forehead, opens the door and ushers you out.

"Our baby's name is Jade by the way. Thought you should know."

When you get home, you wander around. In your home gym, you sit on a balance ball. You turn on the treadmill and watch it spin.

In the bathroom, you grab your packages of birth control. You have never missed a day because there is no excuse for missing a day, unless you were dead or in a coma, in which case you wouldn't be having sex anyway. You lift the toilet lid, twirl the dial and let the days fall.

When Eric comes home, you ask for an update on Mrs. Jamison's eyelashes.

"All accounted for."

"Phew."

He grabs your hand, which is how you know he is about to share a big thought, tell a joke, divorce you.

"I think right now, exchange students are a better idea for us. I'd even go for the seahorses or a couple of Chihuahuas. You could buy them matching coats."

"I can do the baby thing," you say, more or less to convince yourself.

When Eric goes to bed, you stay up and think about the social experiment you did in high school. Everyone was assigned a raw egg baby and was charged with taking care of it for a week. You went home and scrambled yours. The next day, when you told your teacher you had eaten your baby, she started the mock Child and Family Services paperwork.

With no eggs in the house to prove yourself, you get out a small bag of flour and put the Itsy Bitsy sailor dress and frilly underwear on it. You give the sack a happy, impartial, convincing face and glue on some wool for hair.

"I wuv you Gwacie Wacie."

For the next week, you take Grace with you. You shop and run errands on the other side of town. You pull a blanket over Grace's face, shush anyone who tries to talk to you, bare your teeth at anyone who tries to get near the stroller. With more persistent, nosey, bitchy, we're-all-in-this-together mothers, you talk quietly of colic, teething, the convenience of caesarean sections. Occasionally, you have to stick Grace in your purse or desk drawer.

At the end of the week, there is nothing left of Grace but an empty bag. You try again. Grace II. At the end of the week, there is about one cup of Grace left. You're getting the hang of it. You go through a few more Graces until you're ready to strike a deal. You bring Eric coffee in bed and introduce him to your love child. You do not mention the seven sisters that died before her.

"If I can keep her alive for seven days, you have to do me with baby-making intentions. On demand."

He scratches Grace's chin and sips his coffee.

"Okay, but it looks like the baby already has a leak."


After one week of top-notch parenting, Grace has mostly retained her shape and you resubmit her, like a portfolio, for evaluation.

You stand back and watch while Eric inspects her, pausing on the glue and duct taped areas. He wipes his hands, *lightly* dusted with flour.

"I could have made three dozen muffins with this baby last week, now I could only make one."

Before he says anything else, you demonstrate how to change Grace's cloth diaper. You jiggle her up and down. You burp her.

"What more do you want?"


After work, Eric lies in bed waiting—the look on his face a mixture of hope and dread.

"I can't do it with the flour sack watching."

You turn Grace toward the wall.

"You know it's a myth that lying with your legs in the air will help you conceive?" Eric says.

You are negotiating with the baby gods. Convincing them you will fold yourself into whatever post-coital contortions you need to. If they could just send Jade down the pipeline. Pronto.

At work, you make final arrangements for an exhibition opening. You should be briefing yourself on the artist and history of his work. Instead, you read up on what to expect while you are pregnant: hormone fluctuations, morning sickness, frequent urination, an inner glow.

At the exhibition opening, you feel you should mingle. This is your job. You do wonder more and more about the contributors and what makes them support art. Last month the gallery was filled with a bunch of bananas dangling from the ceiling. The artist measured strings and applied a particular knot to each stem. As the bananas ripened, they were removed and made into banana bread. Proceeds from the resulting bake sale were donated to the local food bank.

This exhibition is a bunch of hay bales scattered around the gallery. Several walls had to be removed to accommodate the round ones. In your press release the artist wanted you to stress the importance of scent and placement. "My work is all about symmetry and the spaces in between," he said. "Also, if people want to take a piece of the hay to chew on, they can. These pieces are interactive."

You sip sparkling water and approach one of the guests. "Scent is so evocative, don't you think?" You sniff one of the bales.

"These bales are bullshit," she says, tips her head back and empties her glass.

You are relieved and gesture for her to sit down. She does not want to talk bales. She eats her sushi with a knife and fork and tells you she had to put down her Ragdoll cat because she just bought a leather sofa—like this one, only white. She pets the sofa like it's a big friendly cow. While she tells you how much she liked her Ragdoll—the way he pawed her face in the morning and wanted kibble—all you can think about are nursery colours and peeing on plastic strips.


Tick tock. You have read that visualizing and convincing yourself you are actually pregnant will make it so. To really get into it, you call in morning sickness for the next few weeks.

"Congratulations. I didn't realize you were pregnant," your director says.

"It came on fast," you say.

He says you can work from home if you are up to it, give a shit, want to keep your job. He sends you photos of the next exhibition—a bunch of painted twigs. He includes notes from the artist who has elaborated on the exact position his twigs were in when he found them. Prone on a beach. Vertical in a rubbish bin. Lying in mourning on the sidewalk.

Although Eric objects, you hire a designer for the nursery. A designer who insists on painting in lemon, lime and orange—a sherbet motif. You want to lick the walls every time you come in. When you told him you were having a girl, he insisted on adding his signature castle mural called lullaby princess.

After working with him for a month, he finally asks, "So honey, when are you due? You're flat as a board."

"I'm about three months along," you say, hoping he's working on the final strokes of the knight's jousting spear and you will never see him again.

Jade is coming—she is just fashionably late.

At the doctor's office, you shift in the hard plastic chair and read back issues of women's magazines. You learn all about having an addiction to teeth whitening, the twenty-five minute casserole and last year's new fall colours. You have a male gynaecologist. You try to convince yourself you don't hate this but you do. You try to tell yourself he comes highly recommended but you don't care. When the nurse calls your name, your vagina knows instinctively to clench.

Your doctor is an efficient man who, you are convinced, snaps on those gloves before touching his wife too. As you put your legs in the stirrups, he tells you to scoot closer to the edge and makes hand gestures. "Scoot. Scoot. Scoot."

You inch your way down and do your best to think of last year's new fall colours.

When you get your baby-making diagnosis back, your doctor hands it over like a fish still flopping on a silver platter.

"Many things are working against you."

"Like?"

"You've got a hostile womb, your age, you have an acidic pH and your uterus is tilted and shaped like a heart."

That doesn't sound so bad. Who wouldn't want to spend the first nine months of their life wrapped in a heart?

"See this?" He taps the backlit image and you know you are about to be taught a lesson. "See where the heart cleaves? Less room for a child to grow. It would likely pop out early."

When you get to your car, you search your handbag for your keys but find the Itsy Bitsy Bundt cake instead. It is still wrapped in its little stork-shaped box. The belly is stale and mostly crushed now but you moisten it with your fingertips and try to reshape it. When the little mound can't be put back together, you take a bite of what remains.

At home, you turn into a puddle in Eric's lap. He was such a good sport about masturbating into the cup and rushing it off for testing. You were one hundred percent certain he was the problem. He had stubborn sperm. Lazy sperm. Not enough sperm. New Age sperm that didn't like to compete. Something was wrong with the assembly line. They were all heads. Or tails.

He runs his fingers through your hair and as you explain your hostile womb, you feel like a woman with two hearts—neither works.

You call in miscarriage. You have no choice. You need to reset your babymeter back to zero months. You stay home for a week. When you return, everyone is extra nice but no one says a thing.

You have always pitied couples who say "not yet, but we're trying." So, you keep your efforts quiet but you do keep trying.

Then, at the one-year point, you stop. Order a cease and desist. Only there is nothing to stop except peeing on plastic strips and eating excessive amounts of folic acid. There is no point in taking birth control again since you can't get pregnant. There is no point in stopping sex, you're not an idiot. You just don't have to lie there with your legs in the air and pray to the baby gods. You can stop giving a shit about if and when your eggs have dropped. Basket's empty. You take your ovulation chart off the fridge. It likely wasn't the best foreplay.

The only thing you really have to stop is thinking about her—imagining yourself as a mother. You figure you would have been a terrible one anyway. When you were a kid, your hamster did get lost in the wall.

You fill one of Jade's baby bottles with Chardonnay, go into the nursery and turn off the lights. The mobile above her crib spins and five princesses mock you. You deserve to be mocked. With the stress of trying to conceive you have actually lost weight. You run your hand over your stomach. Your hipbones protrude. Your stomach is concave. You crawl into Jade's crib, suck her bottle and fall asleep.

In the middle of the night, you wake and sit in the crib. Grace VIII is sitting on the change table. You grab her and take her into the garden where you dig a hole. You lay her in it and pull a blanket up to her chin. You want to sing a lullaby or a hymn, something comforting, distracting, mournful. All you can think of is the Itsy Bitsy jingle. "Everything's going to be okay Gwacie Wacie. Yes, it is. Yes, it is."

You slowly cover Grace with dirt and replant the wilting peony.


Inside, there is white flour everywhere but you leave it. It is so quiet in here. You wonder if it is newly quiet or if it has always been like this. You are determined to fill this house some other way. You consider fostering a child, becoming a block parent, studying to be a doula.

You research adoption online. There are crack babies, unwanted babies, babies of teen mothers, unwed mothers, terminally ill mothers. There are special needs babies and older children in foster care with profiles like: *Davey is a smiley, happy-go-lucky fellow. And handsome too! He is doing well in his special education classes but is still having a hard time with grief. Since he hit puberty, he often hits others and has a difficult time controlling his rage. He shows great imagination in the way he acts out. Davey has been in foster care since he was six. He needs a forever home. Adopt Davey today!*

Sorry Davey.

There are also foreign babies: Russian, Ukrainian, Chinese. You decide on twin girls from China and order them online. They will cost approximately $30,000 each. Estimated delivery time: three years.

You decide to drive to Eric's office to tell him about your children from Yangshuo. If he's not available, you'll talk to his assistant or one of the patients waiting in the lobby.

*You think you've got problems?*

You go out to your car and imagine securing your twins into their seats. Wonder where you can buy one of those bumper stickers: *Caution. Babies on Board!* As you pull out of your driveway, you sing the ABCs. You are prepping your children for preschool. You can never start too young and these things get competitive.

While you drive, you see Liang and Mei growing up: teething, mashed food, whole food, diapers, potty training, first words, first steps, bedtime stories, training wheels, Band-Aids, school pictures, matching clothes, non-matching clothes, play dates, bunk beds, separate rooms, bunk beds, baton twirling, summer camp, soccer, horses, trombone and flute, duets, school plays, homework, art on the fridge, first crushes, inappropriate outfits, hidden piercings, insecurities, heartbreaks, the sex talk a little too late, all-girls school, plaid kilts and knee-highs, sneaking out at night, secret codes, cellphone plans, high school graduation.

By the time you get to your turnoff, you are exhausted and the girls are in university, Yale and Harvard. Liang is finishing medicine and will work for Doctors Without Borders. Mei is studying mediation and will broker peace deals in the Congo. They are so modest. You know they didn't get this from you.

You can't change lanes so you take the next exit and circle back. There are signs for the airport and soon you are on your way to pick up your daughters. They came to you a year ago and told you they wanted to return to their homeland to explore their heritage before they started their careers.

They said they were hesitant to ask because they didn't want to offend you—because you had been such a wonderful mother. Because you had given them everything: a good life, ponies, haircuts they don't hate you for. They had been organically fed, drank filtered water, were immunized. They said they had to make this pilgrimage and they had to do it on their own. It was something they had to do for themselves.

Although it wasn't how you had pictured things working out, you knew you had to find a way to live without them, find a way to move on. So you let them go. You sent them off. You wished them well and watched them leave you. You prayed they wouldn't look for their real mother. "She's just DNA!" you wanted to say. You thought about running out onto the tarmac and waving their plane back to the gate. But you let them take off. You let them fly away. You knew it was best for everyone.

You're good that way.

# A BOX FULL OF WILDEBEEST

I'M sitting in my apartment in Japan when mother calls to tell me she's had an abnormal Pap smear. I write down the words Pap smear and wonder how telephone lines work anyway? Are they under the ocean? Is there a big whale swimming over our words? Pap smear. Pap smear. Pap smear.

When I don't respond, she says, "Maybe I should come for a visit?"

While mother talks about deviant squamous cells lining up along her cervix like a firing squad, I tear one paper square out of my shoji screen and look through the hole. I had imagined a life here filled with strolls under cherry blossom trees with my geisha friends. I wanted to see hot tub monkeys hot tubbing in the wild. I wanted to hang out. Put my arm around a hairy shoulder. I was supposed to befriend a Zen master, embrace Buddhism, levitate. While floating and drinking green tea, I would tell other people they had it all wrong.

So far, my vision and reality haven't matched up.

"I might have radiation," my mother says. "Nuke my cervix."

I feel a small earthquake and listen to my dishes rattle. I listen for a tsunami warning and look out my window to see if anyone in my building is leaving for higher ground. All is quiet. No forty-metre waves in sight.

"Yes, now is a good time for a visit."

There is a temple in Kyoto. I can't remember the name and it doesn't matter because there are a million of them in that holy city that sells hand-painted scrolls alongside Hello Kitty telephones. The important thing to know is that there are thousands of teeny tiny steps going up and there are thousands of teenier tinier steps going down. It's as if people's feet are expected to shrink by the time they get to the top, as if the air at a higher altitude in Kyoto has feet-shrinking properties.

Somehow, my mother and I, with our big North American feet, make it to the top. We rub a laughing Buddha belly, choke on incense and admire the view. Before we leave, we buy paper prayers and hang them on a string.

"What does it mean?" I ask a man in my shattered Japanese.

"No good," he says. He sucks wind and waves us away.

My mother undoes her prayer and stuffs it in her pocket. "I knew this place was trying to put a curse on me."

On the way down, I take the teenier tinier steps three, four at a time, daring this country to trip me. When I look back, my mother is navigating each stair slowly, carefully. Her big feet hang over the edge and threaten to topple her. Going sideways is no better; her feet seem as wide as they are long. For a moment, I mistake her expression as *I can do it myself* determination. But when I put on my sunglasses, I realize her look is more *afraid of a broken hip in a foreign country*.

"You remember Ken Wilson's daughter?" she asked me during the Pap smear conversation. "She's over there too. She got run over by a bus in South Korea. Her parents had to charter a plane to bring her home. Poor thing was screaming in agony because those people couldn't set a bone properly."

My mother has always admired Ken Wilson's daughter. Although we often did similar things, she had noble intentions. I was in Japan looking for a kimono and a hot tub monkey while she was in Seoul working in an orphanage. In my mother's head, if I were Ken Wilson's daughter, I would take her hand, slowly guide her down the steps and warn her about the perils of the Asian healthcare system. Instead, I slowly move toward her and know that even if I get there, I'll never quite make it.

I'm sitting in my apartment in Paris when a carrier pigeon lands at my window. I take the note attached to its leg.

*I have lumps on my ovaries. Maybe now is a good time for a visit?*

When my mother arrives, we carry her kiwi-sized tumours up the Eiffel Tower, stroll with them along the Seine. We rest for a while in Notre-Dame. Then we rent bikes, put the tumours in the baskets along with our baguette and go looking for the tunnel Princess Diana died in.

"So sad," my mother says and extends her hand to the ghost of a princess.

"We look like tourists," one of the tumours says.

I suggest we spend the rest of the day at a museum.

"Have it your way," my mother says.

In front of the Mona Lisa, the tumours get lumpier and harder to hold.

"All this way just to see an ugly lady smirk?" one tumour says.

When the tumours get squirmy and grow sick of looking at art in the Louvre, my mother says, "Fine!" Then she packs them into her suitcase along with her French linens and carries them back across the Atlantic, business class.

At Bondi Beach, I come across a conch. I hold it to my ear and hear my mother calling out over the sound of crashing waves. "I only have one ovary left. I better get my good one to Australia, immediately."

When she arrives, we carry the ovary between us to the opera house. We buy it its own seat.

"I never liked Verdi," the ovary says at intermission. It complains about the crowd and perfumed women.

The next day, we swim with it in the ocean. I take it surfing. We catch a wave. We all get massages on the beach. Later, we walk it across the harbour bridge and stop halfway. Despite our pampering, the ovary has become slippery and heavy, says it misses its sister. It is supposed to be getting healthier but has started to sprout hair and teeth. The ovary snaps and grabs hold of my mother's finger.

"Everything turns on me," my mother says.

On the count of three, we throw it in the water and watch it float. It hangs on the surface then disappears. When it finally sinks, she grips the rail for a moment. Then she reaches into her purse and pulls out a calculator and an envelope with all of her receipts in it. She starts adding things up, then says, "With all the money I've spent coming to visit you, I could have built a sunroom."


I'm huddled around my radiator in Moscow when it starts tapping out Morse code. Mother tells me her liver is failing.

"You won't like the language here," I tap back.

"Why not?"

"They speak machine gun."

"But I've already booked my ticket."

"The people here are sad and grey. It will upset you."

"But so much history," she taps.

"And yet, they could only come up with two names for an entire population. Natasha and Alexander."

"Don't forget Nikita and Vladimir."

I meet my mother at the airport with a metal tray. She slaps her liver on it and we walk into the winter night. Her mood is lighter. She seems rosy in the cold wind—a wind that only tries to steal things from me, blow soup from my spoon, swipe at my pockets, lift up my skirt. Large Soviet snowflakes fall as we walk through Red Square, our heads and shoulders conquered. My mother holds the tray out as if she's walking through a cafeteria. The liver wobbles like Jell-O. An old man sits hunched on the steps of Saint Basil's Cathedral and asks, "Can I buy that?"

"This is so Tolstoy," she says and keeps walking. Communism agrees with her.

Outside the Kremlin seems like a strange place to talk about summer camp.

"Remember how happy you were?" she says.

"Actually, I hated having to swing on a rope across that ditch. I prayed I'd fall and break my arm so I could go home. I hated making picture frames with macaroni. I hated making those stupid edible necklaces. I hated the buddy system, because I hated my buddy."

"I see," she says. "That camp was expensive. It was a privilege to attend." She stops to watch a Russian couple talking. All conversations here sound like arguments. "I remember that macaroni frame. You never put my picture in it."

"It was a gift. You were supposed to put a picture in it."

"I'm not sure why you insisted I come on this trip if you're only going to tell lies." She disappears into the snowy night and takes her liver with her.


In a sleeper car on the Trans-Siberian someone knocks on my door. When I open it, the attendant smiles and puts a banana to her ear. I follow her to another compartment. She points to the phone then turns her back as if I'm about to get undressed.

"What if I were dying? What if I were really dying?" my mother asks.

"Are you?" The train rumbles beneath my feet and I brace myself.

"I could be."

"Well, if you were really dying, I'd come home and take care of you."

"I'm going to die alone tits-up in a ditch somewhere."

"Are you dying?" The wind howls through windows that never seem to close properly.

"I just have eczema right now but it's very itchy. Should I meet you?"

"It's freezing in Siberia. It will only make your skin worse."

When I get off the train in Omsk, my mother is standing there in short sleeves, arms outstretched. I'm not sure if it is an invitation to embrace or if she just wants to show me her rash.

"Didn't you bring a proper jacket?" I ask.

"Are you concerned? Are you showing concern for me?"

"Did you come to Siberia without a winter jacket?"

"I wanted to feel what Dostoyevsky felt."

"We're not doing hard labour in a gulag. Have you even read Dostoyevsky?"

"No, but I have a collector's copy of *The Brothers Karamazov*."

My mother is shaking so I give her my coat and we go looking for proper clothes. I try to use her for a windbreak but she says, "It's your trip. You lead the way. Just pretend like I'm not here."

By dim street light, we move toward the shops. There is an eerie beauty here, sad snow that makes a peculiar moaning sound as we walk. The city's streets are unusually wide. Wind gathers speed and goes unchecked. There are rules and no rules. We are blown along. All of the buildings here are oversized to make people feel small and nervous. Every one of them feels full of secrets. Ever since I arrived in this country, I have felt imaginary crosshairs trained on me, as if some KGB spy on a rooftop were going to take me out.

"Honestly, you're so paranoid," my mother says.

At the clothing store we both buy Russian hats and sable fun-fur coats. My own jacket doesn't stand up to Siberia cold. Without looking at me, the storekeeper inspects my roubles with a magnifying glass. When she turns away, I take the coats and hats and quickly walk out.

"Now what?" my mother asks.

We take shelter in a doorway. I grab my map titled *Bird's Eye View of Omsk (pictures made from a plane)* and we march around the city in our matching hats and coats. I read my brochures as we go. "In spring and summer city is filled with beautiful gardens and flovers."

"Flovers," my mother says. "I guess they'd be frozen flovers now."

"Yes, I guess they would." I pull my hat down and brace against a wind so cold it splits my bones.

In the hotel, we sit on our beds and stare at each other, cold and exhausted, still wearing our hats and coats. "How do people live here?" I ask.

"You're omsking the wrong person."

I smile and would love to give that a pity laugh but I'm not that generous.

My mother takes off her hat. "I wish I had been funnier."

We eat dinner at the hotel where we are promised "the aroma alone will dragged you in." The cutlery is heavy and takes two hands to lift. The plates are edged with gold but only the stubborn bits remain. Through the window, I watch two soldiers walk side by side through the snow, heading toward a birch forest. I look again and they are single file. They stop to drink from a flask and have a laugh. White clouds puff out their noses and mouths. The younger one is laughing so hard he falls to his knees and holds his sides. The other points his gun at the fallen one's head. Then he reaches out to help him up. When I look again, they're gone.

After dinner, my mother and I go back to our room. Silent. There is only so much to say about crumbling organs and cracking flesh. My mother strips and can't stop rubbing her arms and back on the red velvet curtains. I pull the ear flaps on my hat down to block out the shush-shushing and fall asleep.

In the morning, I see she spent the night making a ball gown out of the curtains. It actually looks nice—very Russian, but nice.

"This feels so good against my skin."

On our way to the station, my mother—in her hat, sable fun-fur and red velvet curtain—stops to look at her reflection. "Funny," she says and twirls.

We both start to laugh. We get on the train and don't get off until Vladivostok.


In India, I live in a hut with a thatched roof and mud floor. One of the boys from the village brings me a tin can attached to a string.

"Hello," I say.

"My mammogram shows I have a lump. Maybe now is a good time for a visit?"

"I have Giardia. I'm not feeling well myself."

"Well, it's not cancer. I'll bring you some Pepto-Bismol."

It takes hours to get from the airport to my hut outside of Mumbai but my mother, champion sufferer, says nothing as we inch our way forward. Beside a crowded market we have to wait two hours for an elephant to finish taking a nap. While we wait, people try to sell us gold bangles, hoop earrings, beautiful saris and shawls. Small children crowd our tuk-tuk and ask us for pens. The driver ignores us except when the elephant finally gets up and sways its penis back and forth.

"American women," he says, "this will be a good photo to capture with your camera."

My mother has the defective boob in a basket, covered with a cloth like a warm loaf of bread. To let it see, she takes the cloth away.

"Hi boob," I say.

The boob sits in its basket, surveying the situation. It jiggles a bit. The boob doesn't like India at all.

"Remember that time when Rachel Sanders punched you in the stomach and I had to go to her parents' house and I had that big fight with her mother?" she asks.

I open a new package of pens. "I don't remember that at all. I remember you saying if I was kinder, I wouldn't get punched in the stomach by nice little girls."

"Honestly, you have such an imagination."

Indian children are always smiling. "And, I remember you became friends with Rachel's mother shortly after that."

"No, that was much, much later."

"No, it wasn't."

"What are you saying?"

I want these children to tell me how a pen can make them so happy. A pen! "I'm saying you practically congratulated, no, you practically adopted Rachel Sanders after she punched me in the stomach."

"Why must you ruin our vacations like this? Rachel was a nice girl." My mom covers up the boob. "You don't have to listen to this."

The boob doesn't like the pollution in Mumbai, or Agra, refuses to smile for photos at the Taj. I offer it curry, fresh flowers from the market, but it refuses. The boob perks up a little in Varanasi, so we sit with it on the banks of the Ganges where bodies wrapped in colourful silks surround us.

My mother whispers to the boob for a long time. It's hard to say goodbye to a boob. "Did you know you always preferred to suck from this boob when you were a baby?"

"I thought it looked familiar."

My mother walks into the river and dunks the boob. She washes it gently as bodies float by. All around me, fires burn. The strange outlines collapse and cave in on themselves in ways bodies shouldn't. I see my mother press the boob to her chest to see if it wants to reattach. She puts the boob back in the basket and walks to the shore. We gather sticks and build a raft for the boob. We place it in the centre and bind it in place with red silk. We both walk into the Ganges and watch it float alongside, then overtake a corpse.

"It was always a competitive boob," my mother says.


On the Serengeti, elephants rumble past my tent. The woman I'm sharing this tiny space with is a photographer. She calmly looks at images on her camera and tells me that elephant tears are the same chemical composition as ours.

"Why don't they step on us?" I ask.

"I think it's because they know how that would feel."

Over her shoulder, I watch as she flips past images of the lone Syringa tree at twilight, the elusive leopard, a giraffe and its baby reaching for the same branch. When the elephants are gone, our guide comes to our tent and hands me his walkie-talkie. I hear my mother's voice.

"Breaker breaker. I've got carpel tunnel. Maybe now is a good time for a visit? Back over."

"Ten-four. What's your twenty?"

"I'm travelling with a herd of wildebeest. Do you copy?"

"Copy that. When will you be here?"

"10-43 at the watering hole. Something about a hungry alligator."

"Roger. See you in the morning."

"Ten-four that."

"Who was that?" the photographer asks.

"My mother. She's on her way to meet me."

"That sounds really nice. I wish my mother loved me that much." She goes back to flipping through her images.

In the morning, our guide tells me he can't hold up the tour for my mother, who will be joining us as soon as the herd of wildebeest arrives.

"We've got lions to see," he says.

"It sounds far-fetched, but she will be here."

"I'm sorry. We can't wait."

As our jeep convoy starts out, I hear the rumbling of a thousand hooves moving across the plains. Through a cloud of dust, I see my mother riding one of the wildebeest, her single boob bouncing for all it's worth.

As they approach our convoy, her wildebeest stops and kneels down to let her off. She waves goodbye to it with the hand in its little carpel tunnel brace and the beast canters off. "You didn't have to wait for me," she says as she squishes into our jeep.

"Do you have any luggage?" I ask.

"I was travelling by wildebeest. There are weight restrictions."

Our guide stares at my mother through the rear-view mirror and almost crashes into a tree.

"I had to leave all liquids behind. Can I have a sip?" she asks the photographer, reaching for her canteen.

"Have as much as you want." The photographer starts taking photos of my mother with more enthusiasm than a feasting lion.

"Here," my mother gives me the canteen. "Open this. Can't you see I've got carpal tunnel?"

She tries to look natural for the photographer but can't resist posing for a few. When the photographer turns her attention to a lost baby zebra, my mother says, "There, now you'll have something spectacular to put in that macaroni frame."

In Beijing, I'm walking past a cellphone kiosk when the salesman runs after me, taps me on the shoulder and passes me a phone. "It's for you," he says.

I shrug and put the phone to my ear.

"Kidney failure," she says. "Maybe now is a good time for a visit?"

Beside me, a man horks into a spittoon.

"I can hear you nodding," my mother says. "See you soon."

As we walk along the Great Wall, it's hard moving from station to station. The stairs are steep and crumbling, big stones slip out from under our feet, German elbows dig into our ribs. The kidney is bitchy and complains about the heat and crowds. It asks my mother to stop drinking water.

"It's very unappreciative," my mother says, looking directly at me.

We keep climbing. I try my best to slow down, to offer my arm for support, but I'm falling too. The farther we go, the more yellow my mother becomes. Not yellow-yellow, like sun yellow, but mustard yellow with grey undertones, maybe a hint of olive green. She is the shade of yellow no one's mother should ever be.

"I think we should go back now," I say.

"For what? I can be seen from space right now."

"That's a myth. I think you need help."

"Oh, and you're going to help me?"

I watch the step she is on wobble back and forth. "Yes, I'm going to help you." I'm going to give her one of my own kidneys—a replacement part.

I hire a mule and we ride into the village. I draw pictures for the doctor and we are given a mixture of what tastes like red wine and hemp seed. I fall asleep looking at jars filled with turtle shells, dried snakes and long branches.

"Good luck," the doctor says in perfect English.

As my mother starts to go under, she tells me she wishes I had been a doctor or a lawyer. Somebody. "What are you anyway?" she asks. "What am I supposed to tell people you do?"

"Tell them I'm a runner."

The next time I wake, there will be less of me.

After the transplant, we are moved to a real hospital in the city where we recover side by side.

"This is my daughter," my mother tells the doctor, the nurse, the orderly, the janitor, the other patients in the room. "She saved my life. Isn't that the most amazing thing you've ever heard?"

They all nod politely then move on to their next mess. We both keep lifting up the bandages to look at our stitches.

I'm sitting in my old room, in the house I grew up in, when mother calls me downstairs.

"How does That Nurse expect me to eat pizza when I can't swallow properly?"

Her nurse shrugs, points to the can of Ensure and continues changing the bed sheets. "It's liquid. Only sip what you feel like."

"Bullshit," my mother says. "Now there's a pepperoni stuck in my throat." She leans forward, parts her gown and waves me over. "Here, rub my back but don't use your nails." The nurse holds the gown open while I work over my mother's back in gentle circles. "That's so nice, dear. That Nurse doesn't know what she's doing."

Although it is at someone else's expense, I cannot remember the last time she complimented me. Years ago, she told me I had nice eyebrows (this was after I had plucked them all out and had to draw them back on). She also told me I had nice knees, "Normally the ugliest part of a woman's body." And, now, apparently I can rub a back.

"I can't breathe." My mother's voice is raspy. "That Nurse keeps water boarding me."

The nurse slips an oxygen tube over my mother's head and into her nose. I listen to the soft hiss of air.

"I want to be cremated." My mother squeezes my hand. "And I want you to spread me into the water while standing on that bridge in Australia where we had such a nice time. And don't take the lid off the container and just dump me in a big clump. I want to fan out into the water in a graceful arc."

I squeeze her hand. My mother closes her eyes and leans back. As she rests, I say, "It's okay. I'm here. Just like I told you I would be."

She sits up. "You're only here because you ran out of continents."

"There's still Antarctica."

"Just go," she says. "Play with the penguins."

I rub my transplant scar.

"And get the hair out of your eyes. There's a pretty girl hiding in there somewhere. A skinny one too." She coughs and rests her head on her pillow.

"I'm leaving," I say.

"Surprise, surprise."

As I go upstairs, my mother tells her nurse, "My daughter gave me one of her kidneys but kept the good one for herself."

I'm walking through my old house—empty now yet somehow filled with her. In my room, under the bed, there is a box marked *miscellaneous failures*. Inside is evidence of my flunked childhood: the macaroni frame with no picture; my report cards, with low grades highlighted; my letters from camp, with grammar and spelling notations in the margins. Everything is carefully dated and filed. She has been the curator of my shortcomings.

Once I've gone through everything, I consider my options: bonfire, the shredder, cook the macaroni and have lunch. Whatever I do, I know I need to put it behind me. If I don't, it will sprout legs and march beside me everywhere I go.

As I pack everything away, I take deep breaths and admire each piece. "For stick figures, this painting shows tremendous sophistication. While I'm not saying you're Dostoyevsky, this letter does point to wisdom and maturity well beyond your years. Good job."

I pat myself on the back. Give myself a few gold stars. But when the last homemade card for *moter's day* makes its way back into the box, I close the lid and can't tell if I'm inside or out.

# AIRPLANES COULDN'T BE HAPPIER IN TURBULENCE

Ever since Madison watched *King Kong* on TV she's been having fantasies about scaling the Empire State Building with him. That big ape carrying her into the clouds, clutching her like a twig in his leathery glove of a hand. When attacking planes get too close, he lashes out while holding her to his chest. He takes bullets in the face for her.

Her husband, Frank, protects her with the facts. When she tells him she wants to go to New York for her birthday, he grabs his laptop. He is an actuary. She waits for a statistic.

"You want to get pistol-whipped for your birthday?" Frank asks. "There's a 0.28 percent chance."

Madison stretches out on the bed. "Decent odds."

Frank goes into the adjoining bathroom to pluck his one long nose hair, which reappears each spring like a tulip. "I suppose you want a pony, too?"

"Yes, a white one." Madison shudders. She is afraid of horses. Ponies are worse. They are the kneecap-biting form of the horse. "And I want to go to the Empire State Building."

Frank stands in the bathroom doorway touching his stomach rolls. Reading from his phone, he tells her that thirty-seven people have flung themselves off that building. "Did you forget to flush the toilet?" he asks.

Madison is still lying on the bed, thinking about King Kong and the moment he plummets.

"Well?"

"I'm pretty sure I flushed," she says.

"It doesn't look like my shade."

"Maybe someone broke in and peed in our toilet?"

"Odds are low."

Frank returns to the bathroom. Madison thinks of King Kong lying there on the pavement. All furry and ruined.


Madison has never taken a vacation from her marketing job. She gets anxious at the thought of all those days strung out before her, nothing but hammocks and Mai Tais on the horizon. Lately, the thought of spending several days in a row talking to Frank has made her short of breath. They are good together in small doses, but falter when it comes to anything beyond one-line conversations. At Madison's request, her vacation is paid out annually, despite visits from the bubbly human-resources intern, Ginny, who explains the benefits of taking time off.

"Isn't there somewhere special you have always dreamed of going? Machu Picchu, for example?"

"I'll think about it," Madison said last time, and went back to work while Ginny was still sitting there going on about Incan ruins.

When she finally requests time off for her trip to New York, her boss throws a surprise going-away party.

"But it's only for four days," Madison says. "And two of those are the weekend."

"It's wonderful." Her boss grabs her by the hands as if she has just told her that her cancer (which she does not have) is now in remission.

At the party there is a cake in the shape of an apple. Ginny is beaming, as if the vacation were her doing. She points to the banner she's standing under, which reads, *If You Can Make It In NYC, You Can Make It Anywhere.*

When they board the plane, Frank orders drinks.

"Not until after takeoff, sir."

"Consider it a pre-order."

The Air Canada flight attendant does not look at Frank when she speaks. She carries on slamming overhead compartments shut. Madison is certain the woman dreams of lifting her leg and pissing on everyone.

As the plane takes off, Madison sits with her elbows squeezed at her sides. Even with her own husband she can't claim the armrest. She closes her eyes and tries to sleep but can't. To ensure the plane stays in the air, she must stay awake. Years ago she took simuflight training to get over her fear of flying. The program was only a partial success.

*An airplane couldn't be happier in turbulence. The reason you think it's not okay is because you don't realize how happy the plane is.*

When they descend into New York, she tries to imagine what it was like for those people whose plane landed on the Hudson. As she hears the landing gear come down from the fuselage, she wishes Captain Sully were piloting their plane, that steady, soothing voice telling everyone to brace for impact. A voice that could almost convince her it wasn't going to hurt.

"Forty-seven percent of fatal accidents happen during final approach and landing," Frank says.

"That's helpful. Thank you." Madison has never mentioned her simu-flight training to Frank. She did not know him then and figures it would not change things now. They are well past the point of wanting to know new things about each other.

When they get to the luggage carousel, Frank's orange bag torpedoes out first. He has wrapped it in plastic like a bologna sandwich. Madison watches as the bags are collected, but her black one never comes. While they file a complaint with the airline, Frank investigates the odds of losing black luggage.

"Don't tell me," Madison says.

"Okay, but just know they are high. Very high."

As they get into a taxi, Madison hopes her luggage will show up. She wore a velour track suit and Crocs for the flight. In simuflight school they said it was very important not to wear anything restrictive. If her bag doesn't show up, she will have to do some shopping. She is not starting a new decade in Crocs.

When they get to the hotel, Madison calls her daughter, Lily. Frank sits on the bed. He hasn't spoken to Lily since she started experimenting with lesbianism and he posted a sign on the front door on Thanksgiving that read *Cancelled Until Further Notice.*

Madison thought he was outside hanging her wreath made of shellacked persimmons, which she likes to put up during the holidays. She figured a bird hit the window, but it was Lily throwing her pumpkin pie at the door.

"People were meant to procreate," Frank said to his wife. "If everyone were gay, we'd die off. Is that what you want?"

Madison's mother used to tell her, "Honey, when it comes to men, there's always something."

Although Frank's proposal had been unromantic—"There's a fifty-fifty chance you will say no. If you say yes, we have a forty percent chance of divorcing in less than thirty years"—they had been mostly compatible.

On Thanksgiving, Madison explained to Frank that Lily wasn't actually gay; she was just experimenting.

"Hair colour is an experiment. It grows out," Frank said. "Two women necking on my front lawn can be videoed and put up on the Internet for life."

It wasn't just what he said that bothered her. It was the way he clawed at his actuary's tie and loosened it to let the words out. Later that night, while Madison and Frank sat at opposite ends of the table eating cold turkey and stuffing, Lily drove by honking. She had gathered a small group of friends, and they held a mini pride parade in front of the house. There were men in assless chaps and cowboy hats. Rainbows painted on butt cheeks. Two women in wedding dresses threw confetti. The parade circled twice before leaving.

"Happy Thanksgiving, Frank," they shouted.

Madison stood there mentally cataloguing all the reasons Lily couldn't be a real lesbian. She did not wear man jeans with a lumber jacket. All her clothes were tailored. She didn't work for a grassroots organization that churned out badly designed promotional material telling people (in mismatched fonts) to save the estuaries.

"This lesbianism can't be permanent," Madison said. "I have evidence."

The confetti from the pride parade started to work its way onto their lawn and up their driveway.

"There's your evidence," Frank had said.

Madison looks out their hotel window. Below, people pack the sidewalks of Times Square. When Lily finally picks up the phone, she says, "Speak."

"Just wanted to let you know we arrived safely," Madison says.

"It's too bad half a plane can't crash. You arrive safely. Frank? Not so much."

"I wish you would let me fix things."

"Good luck with that. Okay, bye, Mom. I do love you. Happy birthday."

When Lily hangs up, Madison keeps talking. "That's so great, dear. I'm glad it's all working out. Send my best to Patty."

She goes into the bathroom, sits in front of the vanity and looks at the damage forty years can do: crow's feet, laugh lines (ha!), loose skin around her neck. She should have it removed and made into a handbag. Save a lizard.

Frank comes in and rubs her shoulders.

"I think Lily is keeping something from me," Madison says.

"Might be a good thing?" He rubs her shoulders. "New York is waiting."


In the morning, a concierge knocks on the door and returns Madison's luggage.

When she opens it, she realizes it's not her bag. There's no name on the tag, just a business address for a cupcake bakery in Toledo. She can't help but look through it; she's careful at first, then she starts rifling. These are the clothes of the woman she wishes she were. Elegant. Effortless. A take-chargey kind of woman.

She removes her track suit and looks through the bag more carefully. Inside, there's a list of things that go together. "Day 1: Red bauble necklace with nude peep-toe shoes and silk wrap dress." She follows the instructions and puts on this outfit, minus the woman's Spanx. The dress fits as if it were custom-made. Madison feels fabulous, lighter. When she comes out of the bathroom, she takes her itinerary out of her bag. She used to feel proud of her organizational skills until Ginny told her that perfectionists are just people addicted to process. She puts the itinerary in the garbage.

"Let's see where the day takes us," she says.

When they get to Central Park, Frank complains that he needs a hip replacement, so they hire a horse and carriage to drive them around. Madison is nervous but figures the animal is too far away from them to do any real damage. They are on their way to Strawberry Fields when PETA ambushes them.

"Horses don't belong in cities. Shame on you!"

One protestor is dressed as a unicorn. Some hold blow-up photos of mangled horses killed in traffic accidents. Others hold photos of the animals' filthy warehouse living conditions.

"Those horses live in up-and-coming real estate," Frank says to the protesters. "Some people can't say as much."

Madison jumps out of the carriage, ashamed.

"I saw it on *Sex and the City*," she says. "I thought it would be nice."

She explains Carrie and The Russian to the unicorn while making a generous donation. The unicorn thanks Madison, says she understands and, shaking a glittery hoof in her face, tells her not to do it again. Madison is prepared to pay the driver and just walk the rest of the way. But when she turns around, she sees Frank and the horse-drawn carriage trot off to Strawberry Fields without her.

"I won't be bullied by left-wingers," Frank says.

Madison considers going back to the hotel but can't remember the name. She runs after them but is quickly hobbled by Cupcake Lady's shoes. She flags down a rickshaw and jumps in.

"Follow that carriage!"

The rickshaw driver sets down the shafts and looks at her. "Are you kidding me?"

"Sorry. Go as quickly as you are able. I need to pistol-whip my husband."

"Do you have a pistol?"

She shakes her head. The rickshaw driver slowly picks up the shafts again and saunters after the carriage. Madison watches the horse's butt swish from side to side in the distance.

Lily wanted a horse for her fifth birthday but her mother gave her riding lessons at the Pony Corral instead. Terrified, Madison watched from the lounge area as the pony trotted by and Lily shouted, "Again, again!"

She remembers the pony smiling. Do ponies smile? She also remembers when Lily fell off, how she was too afraid to go out and help her. She offered to pay another mother to do it for her.

"What's wrong with you?" the woman asked.

"Ponies freak me out."

"When my Jenny fell into a ravine on Mount Rainier, I instantly got over my fear of heights and tight spaces. We climb almost every weekend now."

"So you won't do it?" Madison asked.

The woman took her money and went out into the arena to pat Lily on the shoulder and dust her off. When she came back inside, she said, "Your daughter is just fine. They're made of rubber at that age. You, on the other hand, need some work."

When she catches up with the carriage, Frank is already at Strawberry Fields paying tribute to John Lennon. The driver is waiting for him.

Madison looks at the white horse, whose name is Steve. He is calm with big, wet eyes. He wears blinkers so he can't see much, and he has nice fluffy feet like those fancy chickens. He doesn't look miserable. He doesn't look like he needs a unicorn to advocate for his retirement.

"Does he really live in a warehouse?" she asks the driver.

He nods.

"How does he relax and stretch out?"

"He does yoga."

When Frank returns, he grabs Madison's hand. "I'm sorry. But this horse isn't suffering. I think you can see that."

"A lot of things don't look like they are suffering." Madison slowly reaches out and pets the horse's neck, making its skin quiver. She gets in and they spend the rest of the day exploring New York in silence.

When they get back to the hotel, Madison calls Lily and gets her answering machine.

"You've reached the newlyweds. Leave a message."

She wants to hang up, wants to track down and assassinate the inventor of caller ID.

"Well, congratulations. I had no idea. I'm so happy for you." *Be casual. People elope all the time.* "New York is wonderful. Frank bought me a brooch from a vintage jewellery shop." She touches her *Vegans Make Better Lovers* PETA badge. "We're having the best time. Anyway, congratulations. I'm going shopping tomorrow. I'm going to bring you home the most fabulous wedding present."

By the time Madison hangs up, she knows Lily didn't elope; she simply didn't invite her.

On the eve of her fortieth birthday, Madison—dressed in another woman's clothes—and Frank go up to the viewing deck of the Empire State Building. A saxophonist is in the corner, playing with his eyes closed. Frank asks him to play *Happy Birthday.*

"Sorry, it's copyrighted."

Frank hands him $100 and the song is suddenly public domain.

After Madison and Frank walk around the perimeter, she goes into the gift shop to buy an *I ♥ NY* key chain. From inside, she watches the people on the deck. A hand-holding lesbian couple are on a collision course with Frank, who, instead of moving out of their way, puffs up like a blowfish—

actually inflates his cheeks—and braces himself. The women don't blink. They unlock hands and walk around him. Then their hands effortlessly find each other again. Madison goes back out to the deck and puts the key chain in the saxophone player's hat.

At midnight, Frank kisses her like old married people kiss—as if they've forgotten where their lips are. If they manage to connect, it is by mere chance.

Before they leave, Madison looks over the edge of the building, hopeful for a moment that Kong is coming.

When they get back to their hotel, Frank pays the cab driver and gets out. He had spent most of the ride reading from his phone, telling Madison about all the things a forty-year-old woman has to look forward to: increased vaginal dryness, bladder problems, mood swings. He is almost at the hotel doors—still talking about estrogen levels—when he realizes Madison is still in the cab.

"Do you know where those carriage horses live?" she asks the driver.

The driver nods. "More or less."

"Take me there."

As the taxi pulls away, Madison enjoys watching Frank follow on foot until she is out of sight. The ride lasts about twenty minutes before the driver stops in a grungy area that smells like rotten eggs and dog shit.

Madison gets out and looks up at a dilapidated warehouse. In a dirty third-storey window she sees the face of a white horse. She tries the door. It's locked, so she goes to the back of the building and crawls through a broken window. Inside there's a freight elevator, but she worries it will make too much noise. She takes the broken stairs instead. As she goes up, she looks through the open doors and cracked windows. The first two levels are abandoned. She has to admit she sees loft conversion written all over the exposed brick.

When she gets to the third floor, the door squeaks open and the horses turn to look at her. They are surprised but not alarmed. When one goes back to eating, they all do. She imagines they went through a desensitization program much like simuflight school. They likely had balloons popped in their faces, babies pulling their lips, little dogs in coats nipping at their ankles.

Madison walks through the dimly lit barn. It is filthy and the horses stand in piles of shit. Their butts are enormous. She looks for Steve and thinks she sees him. She will have to walk past his butt and those tree-trunk legs to untie him. At the park, she never noticed just how thick his ankles were.

"What are you doing?"

Madison turns around to find a man holding a pitchfork.

She puts her hands in the air and says, "I want a pony."

He looks her up and down then lowers his pitchfork. "For what?"

"It's my birthday. Then I'm going to re-gift him as a wedding present."

"You can't just come in here in your high heels and pick a horse."

"These shoes aren't really mine. They belong to Cupcake Lady from Toledo. I normally wear flats. Crocs, in fact."

"Right." The man twirls the pitchfork and looks as if he is contemplating raising it again. "You the lady who followed the carriage yesterday?"

She recognizes the driver. "Yes, that was me. I don't want Steve to live like this. It doesn't seem right. I want to show him what a pasture looks like, open spaces. My daughter knows how to look after horses. She had training at the Pony Corral."

"You should go save a whale or something." He keeps looking at her, twirling the pitchfork as she slowly takes off her wedding and engagement rings. They are each one-carat diamonds and look beautiful in any light, even a damp warehouse. Then she empties and hands over Cupcake Lady's handbag.

"The bag is worth almost as much as the rings," she says.

"No kidding." He admires the bag.

"Sell it on eBay. Describe the leather as *coffee*, not brown."

"You can't have Steve. He's my friend."

He unties a different shit-stained horse and backs it out of its stall. Big patches of its head are yellow, like faded newspaper.

"This is Sarge. He's retired and by retired I mean he goes to slaughter next week."

"People eat horses?"

"Europeans and Japanese do. Apparently it tastes like a cross between chicken and cotton candy."

Sarge's feet are the size of anvils. She worries he will crush her. The floorboards groan under his weight, but he looks too sleepy and ready to retire to do anything malicious. Madison decides no one is going to eat Sarge.

The man hands Madison her horse's rope. She pulls, but Sarge won't budge. The man makes a clucking sound and the horse moves forward.

"Does he come with anything? A leash? A small bag of food?"

"Sold as is. How far do you plan on taking him?"

"Canada."

"Of course."

When the freight elevator comes up she goes inside, but again Sarge will not follow.

"He doesn't want to leave his friends. They're herd animals. This is all he's ever known."

"If he doesn't leave, he'll die."

"True," the man says. He walks beside the horse and makes the clucking sound again. Sarge moves forward.

"Can you teach me how to make that sound?"

They stand and cluck. When Madison thinks she has it down, she asks, "What do you think of gay people?"

"I like 'em just fine. Long as they keep their shit to themselves." The man still has her purse thrown over his shoulder and is wearing her rings halfway on his pinky.

Outside, a police siren whines. Somewhere other people argue. When Madison thinks she has the cluck down, she gets in the elevator.

"What will I do once I get outside?" she asks.

"I suppose you should have thought about that."

Before the doors close, the man offers to call a friend who could meet them with his trailer at a gas station. Madison will have to walk with Sarge, her $6,000 horse, for almost twenty blocks. She agrees but has no idea if they will make it or if the friend will really be there.

"What about paperwork for the border?" she asks.

"Again, you should have thought about that."

The doors close. Madison formally introduces herself to Sarge. "I don't normally do this kind of thing."

When they get to the bottom floor, the elevator doors open halfway then jam. Sarge gets antsy. Madison prays he will behave. She does not know how to negotiate with a horse.

The doors shut and the elevator goes up. When the doors open partway, they are between floors. The other horses move somewhere above them. Sarge paws the floor and seems anxious to rejoin them. Madison would kill for a gin and tonic. She pounds the red emergency button, which does nothing but beep and make the horse more nervous.

The elevator doors close again, and they go back down. Madison listens to the doors trying to work; they click and grind as if sensing her indecision.

She pulls out her phone and makes a call.

"The Cupcakery. Make every day your sweetest."

"Am I speaking with the shop owner?"

"Owner. Operator. Baker. Chief decorator. Two-time state champion runner-up for my red velvet cupcakes."

"How did you feel about coming in second?"

"Kind of pissed. They said there was too much vanilla in my frosting and the amount of sprinkles I used was garish."

The elevator starts going down. With the doors slightly open, Madison can see the vacant floors as they pass. Hollowed out spaces where people used to have lives before the horses moved in. "Will you try again?"

"The whole thing is rigged, but I'm not going to let some sprinkles keep me down."

Sarge flares his nostrils and takes short breaths. The elevator stops. The door opens wide enough for Madison to see they are on the ground floor. She pries the doors open.

"Would you like to place an order?" Cupcake Lady asks.

Madison looks at a stack of crates and contemplates how she will get on the horse.

"We've got mocha minicakes on special."

Madison considers telling her she will stop by when she returns her luggage. That they can share a mocha minicake then. But she knows she will never be in Toledo.

"Good luck at the bake-off. This is your year. I can feel it."

She hangs up. Sarge nuzzles against her shoulder. He is actually cute in a worn-out way.

She tries to position him close to the crates. She is mostly on top of him when she lifts her leg over, tearing her skirt and spooking the horse. He trots forward down the lane, with Madison hanging off the side of his neck. When they get to the first traffic light, Sarge stops on the red, and she both swings and wills herself onto the horse.

"Nice moves," someone yells from a window above.

Once Madison rights herself, the light turns green and the horse clip-clops forward.

"You're a gift for my daughter. She's going to love you."

Sarge's ears rotate like satellite dishes as Madison talks to him. They pass parks and tall buildings. The horse seems to have a route in mind. Madison admires his sense of duty. She tries to relax and loosen her grip. Whenever she is about to slide off, he stops and waits for her to adjust. She tries not to think about odds and whether they are in her favour. When she clucks, the horse moves forward.

# DOWNWARD SLUMP IN THE PRODIGY MARKET

At her preschool interview, Tulip stared at the dancing hippos painted on the wall. She knew hippos were not purple and would never wear tap shoes. She worried about the school's curriculum—saw Popsicle stick art and finger painting in her future.

"I'm here to interview you, too, you know," she said. "There are plenty of other preschools in the area."

From the corner of the room, Tulip's mother, Anne, gnawed on her bottom lip. While it was true, there were other preschools, a few botched interviews meant only the private options were left. The girl had a musical ear and all she wanted to do was play the piano or tap out rhythms.

"I'm the soundtrack to your life," Tulip would say when asked to stop banging on pots.

If her daughter didn't get into this school, she would be a year behind the other kids. Her file would say *late bloomer*.

"Don't pull a stunt," Anne said, immediately regretting it. She didn't want the teacher to think pulling stunts was a regular thing.

"Relax, Anne." Tulip refused to call her parents mom and dad. "*I basically parent myself.*"

The teacher sighed and put down the child's resumé, which Anne had fluffed up a bit.

"Tell me about your volunteer activities. How do you make the world a better place?"

"I help feed the shut-ins at Christmas," Tulip said in a robotic kind of way.

"I see you like music. Let's sing the alphabet backwards and forwards."

Tulip knew preschool was going to be a big waste of her life but she sang anyway. If she didn't get in, she would have to be homeschooled. She knew two homeschooled kids. They didn't wear shoes, wore clothing made of natural fibres and went door to door trying to sell their chickens' brown speckled eggs. These kids also tried explaining that God invented dinosaurs and, although it was a tight squeeze, they too fit onto Noah's ark.

Tulip could only imagine what Anne's curriculum might look like so she did what she was told.

"Do you have a piano?" Tulip asked. Her fingers played out chords on the desk.

The teacher shook her head.

"Fine, I'll sing a capella. I guess this isn't Carnegie Hall."

After the ABCs and CBAs, Tulip was asked to hop around the room, pour a glass of juice and stand on one foot for thirty seconds while touching her nose. Then she was supposed to draw a rainbow to demonstrate her knowledge of colours, but she couldn't stop looking at the hippos. She got up and drew a frown over one of their mouths.

"She wouldn't smile like that if she were forced to dance," Tulip said. "I'm just being realistic."

The teacher wrote *caution: not ready to be a learner* in Tulip's file and granted her conditional entry. "She's very combative," she said to Anne. "Maybe you could work on that?"

Anne nodded, signed the paperwork, wrote the cheque and ushered her daughter out of the room before the teacher could change her mind.

At dinner, Anne told her family about Tulip's successful entry into preschool. Tulip's eighteen-year-old sister, Lena, who was destined for beauty school, listened with great interest.

"Who draws on a hippo?" she asked and kicked Tulip under the table.

Tulip knew it was irrational to admire her sister. A future hairdresser! Still, she wanted to ask Lena about her messy bun. How it was both messy and perfect at the same time. She wanted to know about gel-filled nails and whether she could still play piano with them, but Tulip just rubbed her shin.

"She got into the program. That's the most important thing," Anne said as she cut Tulip's tuna steak into bite-sized pieces (she didn't like the girl using her hands unless she absolutely had to).

With nothing to do but wait until Anne stuck a fork in her mouth, Tulip smiled and asked her father, "Why don't you play piano, Barclay?"

"He's not gifted like you," Anne said. "He's just a carpenter."

Barclay, who did not like having to pay for preschool, sat there cutting his own steak, trying to think of the best way to outsmart his daughter. He often rehearsed. He had to. She had an answer for everything.

"Did you know Thomas Edison only went to school for three months?" he asked.

No one said anything. He was disappointed with his delivery. Too forced. Too obvious. It sounded much better in his workshop with the band saw whirring. He wanted to be casually superior. *No big deal. I'm just smarter than you.*

Tulip took a small bite of her steak, chewed thoughtfully then said, "Thomas Edison was a very cruel man who publicly electrocuted an elephant. Her name was Topsy."

"Isn't that sad," Anne said, looking at her husband. "Poor Topsy." She cut the steak, screeching the knife across the plate with every swipe. "If Thomas Edison had stayed in school, he would have probably learned that electrocuting elephants was wrong. I think they cover that on the first day."

Barclay made a cross with his knife and fork and laid them across his plate. He went to his carpentry workshop where the sound of power tools and his fingers close to the blade relaxed him. His specialties were pergolas and arbours—things that made sunny places shady.

After dinner, Tulip went out to her father's workshop. She wanted to tell him that, throughout Topsy's life as a performer, she had had sand thrown in her face, her trunk burned with a cigar, and she had been stabbed with a pitchfork. This is why she misbehaved. Tulip thought these were important details.

Tulip stopped at the doorway. She had grown up with the whir of a mitre saw in the background, always cutting her thoughts and sentences and songs in half. Still, the sound of the blade tearing through wood always made her nervous.

Her father sometimes invited her in. Had dreams of whittling with his daughter. But the doorway was as far as she could go. Today, when he saw her, he took his eyes off the blade for a moment and the tips of three fingers flew past Tulip's head.

On the first day of preschool, when Tulip was asked to introduce herself, she said, "My name is Piano."

Her teacher did not call her Piano; she called her an underachiever because all she wanted to do was sit and rock. Anne explained that sitting and rocking wasn't an actual class and she would have to try harder at other things.

"And cutting off Barclay's fingers was not your fault," she added.

Her mother's lectures did no good. When confronted with any kind of test, Tulip simply wrote *irrelevant* in red crayon, handed it in and said, "Yes, I'm prepared to let you fail me."

At the school talent show, while some kids went on stage and attached spoons to their faces, Tulip approached her instrument fearlessly and played

Beethoven's *Hammerklavier*. While she had heard of stage fright, she figured it must be something that happened to other people. She just let her mind go blank, touched her fingers to the cool keys and let the piano play her.

For Barclay, buzzing from painkillers, it was the first time he had heard her play an in-tune piano with no missing keys. He had always disagreed with Anne about the level of Tulip's talent. Anne called Tulip an undiagnosed prodigy and felt it was just a matter of time before Oprah came calling. She even had an MRI of the kid's brain stuck to the fridge with a magnet that said *beat that!*

"Check out that corpus callosum," she would say to family and friends.

As Tulip continued to play effortlessly, even Barclay had to admit she was good—maybe better than good. When she finally stopped playing, he thumped his bandaged hands together until they throbbed.

The next day, Tulip and her parents met with the school psychologist who apologized and said Tulip had been mislabelled. She was not a combative underachiever; she was a selective consumer.

"It's a good thing," the psychologist assured Tulip. "Have you always played so well?"

"I don't play. I just help the piano express itself," she said.

"Okay." The psychologist made a fury of notes.

Soon, Tulip was gifted. Soon after that, her paperwork was expedited and she was officially a prodigy. The principal recommended she attend prodigy school—a holding pen for prodigies until they could be released into their respective Ivy League schools or start their careers as miniature nuclear physicists or concert pianists.

At night, Anne whispered to her husband, "Should we try making another?"

Barclay shook his head. Tulip was either a fluke or they had taken home the wrong baby. But Anne dreamt of starting a prodigy factory and tried seducing her husband at every opportunity, which wasn't easy when he whispered things like *did you know vibrators were originally used to treat female hysteria in the nineteenth century?*

But Anne had an entrepreneurial spirit.

At prodigy school orientation, Anne and Tulip listened to the coordinator's spiel. Once happy just to get Tulip into any school, now Anne said things like, "I will not let you waste my daughter's talent by assigning her busy-work!"

The coordinator said, "We take for granted Tulip already knows how to nap, count to ten and make a stamp out of a potato."

"Good. That's good," Anne said.

"But we do try to educate well-rounded prodigies here," the coordinator continued. "Too many of our graduates were ending up living under the I-95."

When she reported back to Barclay, she assured him of their daughter's imminent success as a world-famous concert pianist.

"Think of it as an investment," she said as she showed him the tuition fee schedule (payable in twelve easy instalments).

When Barclay tucked Tulip in at night, he rubbed the pads of her fingertips with his gauzy hands and kissed each finger goodnight. *Ka-ching* he thought and insured Tulip's hands the next day.

"It just makes good business sense," he said.

Tulip wasn't sure she was a wise investment but her father's excitement and interest in her life ignited a strange feeling, which, she guessed, must be pride or something like it.


As Tulip prepared to leave for prodigy school, Barclay spent more time listening to his investment play. They had little savings and not being able to use his hands meant it was dwindling quickly. If he ever wanted to retire, he would need a nest egg. Instead of monitoring the stock market, which he didn't really understand, he marvelled at Tulip's hands, the masterful way they worked the keys. All this time worrying about money and his pension plan was living right under his roof.

As she played, he offered helpful comments such as "way to go" and "that sounds just like a real song."

Tulip was nervous now playing with her father standing right behind her all the time. He messed up her timing by tapping his foot, as if she were playing a jig, not Chopin. Before, when she started practicing, she could always count on her father going to his workshop to be with his saws and to, as he put it, "escape all the racket." Now, as soon as she started to play, he would come running and grab her hands, saying, "There are twenty-seven bones in here. Work your magic."

When Lena discovered the insurance payout would be over half a million dollars, she tried to pulverize Tulip's hands.

"Why wait for her to start making money at concerts?"

Tulip's last days before moving to prodigy school were spent avoiding slamming doors and dodging textbooks that seemed to fly out of nowhere.

"You're worth more to us handless," Lena said as she chased Tulip around the house.

Her last nights at home, Tulip had a hard time sleeping. She clutched her plastic bust of Beethoven to her chest and prayed she would never have to come back here. She needed her own apartment, filled with frying pans and a can opener, dishes and a bath mat, maybe an industrial grade waffle maker. She doubted Beethoven wasted his energy hoping for cutlery and stemware, but he probably didn't have a sister like Lena. Tulip made her mother sleep outside her bedroom door for protection. Even then, she thought she heard Lena digging through the wall with a spoon.

On the day of the move, Anne dressed Tulip in her new prodigy uniform—a long velvet dress with a wide satin bow around the waist, patent leather shoes and white ankle socks with lace trim. She curled Tulip's hair into ringlets, applied circles of rouge to her cheeks. Though not part of the official uniform, Tulip had to wear falconer's gloves when she wasn't playing her instrument.

"It's part of the insurance terms," Barclay explained.

On the way there, he said, "Get really good soon. I'm too old for compound interest to be of any use to me."

"No pressure," Anne said.

At prodigy school, Lena tried one last time to slam Tulip's hands in the car door. When it didn't work, Lena rolled up the window and sat there picking her nails.

Barclay snapped a Polaroid of Tulip's hands for insurance purposes.

Anne said, "Have fun. Learn lots," and tried not to sniffle.

Tulip couldn't wait to step through the school's front door. When she did, she was welcomed by the head mistress, who shooed her parents away.

"She needs to focus." The head mistress was tall and had a severe haircut with blunt bangs that never moved. "Your life begins right now," she said.

Tulip was led into the school where the other students were all standing around in their prodigy uniforms—tuxedos with tails and top hats, white lab coats and oversized glasses, more long velvet dresses. The violin player was massaging her neck cramp. The linguist was teaching a small group how to say *shit* in twelve different languages.

Tulip was shown to her dorm room.

"Your roommate, Bea," the head mistress said, "is a math prodigy. She was born with a fascination for square roots but lately all she wants to talk about is Snoopy, Ponzi schemes and the imminent collapse of the world economy."

Tulip opened the door. Bea was standing on her bed writing algorithms on the wall in black Jiffy marker.

"I'll keep these on my side," she said without looking back. "I hope the smell doesn't bother you."

Tulip unpacked her things: a nightgown, her bust of Beethoven, toiletries she had stolen from Lena. When she turned around, Bea was sitting cross-legged on the bed, staring at her.

"So? What's your gift?" Bea's pupils were dilated and she had a hard time focusing on one thing for more than a few seconds.

"Piano. You?"

"Math. Are your hands insured?"

"Yes, are you insured?"

"My head is. I'm supposed to wear a helmet at all times but, clearly, I refuse."

Bea helped Tulip remove her heavy leather gloves.

"They can't see you anymore, you know. Even when you're done with prodigy school, you'll probably live in Vienna. We don't have to listen to our parents anymore. As long as we get famous before the crash."

Bea circled a spot on the wall and said, "This is when it happens." Then she got off the bed. "And I knew you were a piano player. I've seen your audition tapes. You've got a lot of work to do before then."

Although she should have been insulted, Tulip felt like she had just played *Flight of the Bumblebee* flawlessly. It was a foreign feeling but she figured this must be what making friends feels like.

At their first assembly, the performers were assigned agents. Tulip sat down with Tabitha to discuss an Oprah special and the late-night talk show circuit. Although these engagements didn't pay, they would create buzz, help Tulip network and establish her brand. Of course, there would be free airfare, hotel accommodations and gift baskets. Lots of gift baskets.

Then, as a group exercise, the performers worked on the exaggerated prodigy bow—dislocate from the waist, bend all the way to the floor, once, twice and, if they were really cute, thrice.

Afterward, in their dorm room, Tulip and Bea talked about the future. While Tulip practised her bow in the mirror, she wondered what it would be like to be fussed over in the green room. Bea's eyes glazed over. She got on a chair and started writing on the wall.

"My advisor is telling me Harvard and a teaching position are sure things. I'm saying it's not going to happen. It can't." She circled another spot on the wall. "This is where it ends. Make sure Tabitha books your appearances before the crash."

"Will do," Tulip said.

She thought Bea was either a brilliant oracle or a bit of a loon. Either way, she was growing very fond of her. When Bea was done with her doom-and-gloom predictions, they went to the cafeteria for dinner where they stopped and stared at the vats filled with overcooked broccoli, bananas and green tea.

"Brain food," the cook said as he slopped it on their trays.

Each night, Tulip's family called her and spoke into their phones at the same time.

Barclay asked how his investment was doing. "Are you wearing your gloves? Your insurance isn't cheap, you know."

"We miss you, honey," Anne said. "Just have fun. That's the main thing."

"It's not a badminton game," Barclay countered.

Lena told her sister she had secret agents working inside the prodigy school. "Don't get too comfortable. Especially late at night."

Tulip hoped at least one of Bea's predictions would come true: she would move to Vienna. She had always wanted to leave home, but she hadn't considered leaving the country—putting an entire ocean between her and her family.


After their assessments, the prodigies were given private teachers. Tulip was assigned to Ivan. Like most of the faculty, he was a washed-up prodigy who had taken part in various prodigy rehab programs. They found him during a prodigy round-up, living under a tarp near the river where he had collected a family of cats whom he often fed before feeding himself. Ivan, like the other teachers, felt uncomfortable with his charge, threatened by youth and talent, by possibilities that were behind him now.

The head mistress assured Tulip, "His heart is in the right place and Hallmark is considering optioning his story for a movie of the week. Talking cats. The whole bit."

For most of her lessons, Ivan offered muffled (though helpful) suggestions from the corner of the room where he stood facing the wall. When Tulip felt too stressed out, she would say something like "I'm having difficulties with the phrasing in *Minuet in A*. What do you recommend? I'm going on Breakfast Television in a few weeks, you know."

Uncomfortable with being put on the spot, Ivan would cough his way out of the room and say he'd be right back. Then Tulip would go to the bathroom with the best acoustics, stand on a toilet seat and listen to people pee. She found this shameful but relaxing and it posed all kinds of interesting research questions:

Could the calculus prodigy really never remember to flush? It's just one step.

Could the cello player really be holding that much piss and still look dignified while playing Bach?

At the Breakfast Television studio, Tulip was accompanied by Tabitha and Ivan. Ivan was going to say a few things about Tulip. When the producer saw him walking backwards and talking to himself, she cut him.

"Sorry, kid. It's all you now," she said.

Tulip was just glad Ivan was there, advising her until the last minute. When she went on stage, she let her mind go blank, approached her instrument fearlessly, touched her fingertips to the cool keys and let the piano play her.

That night, she had close to 500,000 hits on YouTube. Her Twitter account bulged with encouragement from fans: *My son was supposed to be on that show. He sings the anthem doing burps. I think you stole his spot.*

Tulip tried not to let it go to her head. Her father wanted to know if 500,000 hits translated into $500,000.

The rest of Tulip's appearances were just as successful. Only the Oprah special was left. Bea assured Tulip she was peaking at the right time.

As the Christmas holidays approached, Tulip received a rubber hand in the mail. The note dangling from one of the fingers read *Happy Ho Ho. Love, Lena.*

Tulip couldn't bear the thought of going home so, while humming *The Nutcracker*, she told her family an engagement at Carnegie Hall had popped up.

"Well, Merry Christmas then, Mozart," Barclay said.

"I'm sure you'll have a nice time," Anne said. "What have you been learning at prodigy school?"

"We learned how to bow and smile gracefully with no front teeth."

"That will be useful," Anne said. Then she broke the news she had been hoping to tell her in person: she was pregnant. Tulip's success was needed now more than ever. "No pressure."

On Christmas Eve, Tulip gave Bea a package of Sharpies. In the morning, she was writing on their dorm room window, slowly blocking out the light. Tulip was disappointed the formulas now covered all four walls, which meant, at some point in the night, Bea had been standing over her while she slept.

"Move your bookings, Tulip. It's almost here." Bea circled a new place on the wall. "Downward slump in the prodigy market. Talent and timing don't always align."

The moment of doom was always circled on a different spot on their wall. Tulip pointed this out to Bea, who turned to her and asked, "You believe in me though, right?"

Tulip was no longer sure. She said yes but felt Bea had officially entered what all prodigies fear: the babbling phase. Tulip knew she should get her some help but she also needed to get ready for her performance, which was hard when Bea kept her up all night with market updates. When Tulip did sleep, she dreamt she would walk onto Oprah's set and play *Hot Cross Buns*. To the millions of viewers at home, she would stand up and say, "I fooled you."

A few weeks before Oprah, Tulip's hands started to shake. She asked Tabitha to schedule a few smaller performances. It had been a while since she had played in front of an audience.

"No time," Tabitha said and got Tulip a prescription for beta-blockers instead. "Sorry, kid. You don't make money, I don't make money."

For her friend's own good, Tulip asked the head mistress to move Bea to the babbling wing—a heavily padded and secure area where her access to Sharpies would be restricted, where her audience would be limited to other babblers who may or may not be geniuses. It was a bit of a grey zone.

"Just until Oprah is over," Tulip said. "Please, I need some sleep."

Although the babbling wing was padded, Bea's voice permeated the halls with muffled warnings. She criticized people for taking on too much debt, for not knowing how to calculate interest. She predicted the housing bubble was about to burst. "Ka pow!" She pounded the walls.

When the markets did crash, she was released and treated like a mini-prophet. Governments, think tanks and investment groups wanted to hire her. Since Bea had free rein at prodigy school, she wanted to stay awhile longer. Every morning, she got on the PA system to announce that all prodigies, like the rest of the world, would have to scale back, reduce expectations, car pool, kiss their pensions goodbye.

"Performers," she said, "can safely assume their bookings are as good as dead. Who cares about the next Yo-Yo Ma when their home is about to go into foreclosure? No one. That's who."

Not even Oprah. Tulip's appearance was cancelled and replaced by a special segment on extreme couponing.


Tulip approached Bea, who hadn't spoken to her since her release, and cautiously asked, "Do you have any idea how I can get my appearance on Oprah rebooked?"

"Nope and I know you're the reason I was incarcerated."

While Tulip had many talents, lying was not one of them. "I'm sorry," she said. "I just wanted some sleep and the details of the crash were always changing. Every day there was a new date."

"You're a good pianist, Tulip. But you're not that good," Bea said. "You should ask your agent to pimp you out to kiddie birthday parties. Get some hot dogs and ice cream out of the deal. Maybe you could get lounge work?"

Tulip watched Bea walk away and knew this is what it felt like to lose a friend.

Each morning, until she left for a position on CNN, Bea got on the PA system with a special inspirational message: "Buck up, prodigies. Buck up."


While speaking to her parents, Barclay talked about work slowing down. Although his coordination would never be the same, he had managed to start working with his seven remaining fingers. But no one needed a pergola and shady places to sit when they couldn't feed their family. They had to sell their second car. Though no one mentioned it, Barclay had cancelled Tulip's hand insurance. Lena was working at a restaurant to help pay for beauty school tuition. Anne wasn't helping matters with her strange cravings for expensive foreign foods she had never even tasted. *"The baby needs dragon fruit. I can't explain it."*

"But we've still got Oprah," Barclay said.

Tulip let Barclay's ramblings about Oprah go on for as long as she could but eventually, she had to tell him her appearance had been cancelled.

"Rescheduled?" her father asked.

"Cancelled. The end. Fini," Tulip said. "I was replaced by coupons."

No longer able to afford tuition, Tulip's family drove to prodigy school where they fought with the head mistress for their daughter's release. Eventually they had to extract her through the window in the middle of the night. Although it was only so she wouldn't fall on her face, it felt good to look down and see her parents' hands reaching out for her.

As they hustled to the car, Barclay stopped and looked at Tulip in her pyjamas and long leather gloves. Instead of telling her she no longer needed them, he rambled on about falconry.

When they got to the car, he said, "So? No word from Oprah?"

"No word from Oprah," Tulip replied as she crawled into the back seat. As they drove away, she looked back at prodigy school and saw Ivan standing in the window. She waved and knew he wanted to wave back but couldn't.

On the dark ride home, Tulip reached around the front seat and pressed her hand to her mother's stomach. Tulip could feel the baby kick in perfect four-four time and she gently tapped back.

While Tulip and her family rode out the volatile market, they knew maturity for a prodigy was a death sentence. At night, they upped her anti-aging regimen. Anne slathered Oil of Olay all over Tulip's face. She encouraged her to relax her facial muscles whenever possible.

"Don't worry about a thing," she said while rubbing Retin-A into Tulip's temples.

They dipped her hands in paraffin wax and wrapped them in mittens. They rubbed Bag Balm on her feet to ensure her heels wouldn't crack. (Tulip noted this cream was intended to sooth animals' chafed udders.)

"You're still daddy's little cash cow," Barclay said. "Things will turn around."

But from behind the little cucumbers they placed over her eyes, Tulip had dreams in which Vienna faded from view.

Although it was ancient, missing keys and always out of tune, Anne sold Tulip's piano on kijiji. As it rolled out the door, Tulip felt like she was losing another friend.

"Don't worry. We'll use the money to buy a new one," Anne said.

But Tulip watched her mother squirrel away the money in an envelope and take it directly to the bank. Tulip had rifled through the stacks of unpaid bills on the kitchen table and knew there was no shortage of things that needed to be paid, including prodigy school tuition, for which they were not entirely off the hook.

In the receivables pile, Tulip noticed Lena had started sending them money. She was so good at beauty school they put her in the accelerated program and allowed her to start taking clients.

Bea was still on the news—the go-to girl for all things crash-related. Her hair had been tamed. Her eyes could maintain focus; the pupils were no longer dilated. She wore a mini-power suit and played with the buttons while she spoke.

During the call-in portion of one show, Tulip dialled the number on the screen.

"What's your question?" Bea asked.

"You look so normal," Tulip said.

"I got out." Bea seemed to know exactly who she was talking to.

Tulip twisted her worn velvet dress in her hand, suddenly aware of how short the sleeves had become, how thin the material was now. "My family and I are still waiting."

"For what?"

"For the markets to improve. For people to care about the prodigies again."

"Not going to happen," Bea said, while twirling around in her chair, wrapping her microphone cords around her chest. "You're done. Why not just get on with real life and stop babbling?"

Tulip smiled her no longer toothless smile. Then, because she didn't know what else to do, she bowed at the waist and hung up the phone.

Tulip called Ivan, but the school secretary said he had moved back to the bridge.

"Which one?" Tulip asked.

"The one with water running beneath it. Look for the cats."

Then Tulip called Tabitha. At the very least, she needed to make enough money to get her piano back. She was willing to play birthday parties, to play for an audience too busy whacking a piñata or chasing the family chocolate Lab to notice her at all. But Tabitha's agency was closed for business.

Tulip put down the phone, stood where her piano once was and moved her fingers through the air until she thought she heard music.


Tulip entered her father's workshop. She watched her father push a cedar beam through the whirring saw, mesmerized by how close his fingers and half fingers were to the blade. Her father was good with his hands too. Doing what he was good at, his face softened, he seemed sure of himself. He had nothing to prove.

After the board split and crashed to the floor in two equal pieces, Barclay stopped the saw. "Something wrong?"

"Anne's craving eggplant pizza."

"She doesn't even know what an eggplant tastes like."

"Apparently the baby does," Tulip said.

Barclay laughed and removed his safety goggles. Tulip watched him disappear inside the house, then let her mind go blank and walked toward her father's instrument.

"There are twenty-seven bones in here," she said. "You're daddy's little cash cow. Things will turn around."

Then she turned on the saw, watched it spin, kissed the tips of her fingers, put them to the cool blade and let it play her.

# YOU CRY UGLY

When a woman has two children she thinks she will love them equally. She prepares for her heart to split. Over time she learns a heart does not divide fifty-fifty. The same applies to grandchildren—a heart cannot be quartered, though some think it can. At Christmas, they make neat piles of the exact same things, wrapping them identically so no one appears favoured. Same paper. Same bow. They tally expenses to make sure one child did not get more than the other. Something is added or taken away.

Although I loved my husband, he was like this. Constantly making love into a fraction. My love has always been on more of a sliding scale. At the moment, my love for my children looks like this: Teddy (87%) and Janie (13%). My love for my grandchildren is like this: Gregory (63%), Leigha (21%), Ryan (13%) and Ophelia (≤ 3%). Give or take. At Christmas there are mountains and molehills and I do not care. I rarely see them and have never met Ophelia. Her gifts sit in the closet for one year and are then donated to Goodwill. So be it. She never got her sock puppet. I'm guessing she lived.

I'll soon find out, as Ophelia is coming to stay with me for the summer because her mother, Janie, decided heroin would be interesting. While my son Teddy is no saint, at least embezzlement is a white-collar crime. It also didn't come as a complete surprise. He always did want more pocket money.

While Janie was known for making an ass of herself at parties, I never expected heroin. I thought someone's pool boy would find her one morning, floating with a highball glass still in hand. I didn't wish this on her. I just felt it was inevitable that an autopsy would reveal excessive amounts of alcohol, chlorine and cucumber sandwiches in her system. In my mind, heroin is reserved for prostitutes, not debutantes—even if she did insist on wearing a dog collar to her coming out party.

In preparation for my time with Ophelia, a friend suggested I watch Music Television and take notes. It was educational, though when Ophelia arrives, it is doubtful I will welcome her to my mad crib or invite her to pimp my ride. I do suspect she will get all up in my grill.


At the bus station, she was to meet the car I sent. I kept sending it for a week and then stopped. A small part of me (≤3%) was curious. I know very little about her. All Janie would say is, "She's a bit of an idealist." Nice work if you can get it.

Weeks later, when she does show up, it is late evening. A motorcycle rips up my driveway and then tears away, rattling my china. Wedgewood complains.

Ophelia stands in the driveway assessing my home, possibly casing the joint. She wears a sweater with the hood pulled up. She looks like the type to write a manifesto. Although she is lithe, she looks like she could bitch slap or car jack someone if needed. Perhaps she carries a bomb in her back pocket—should the right cause and garbage can present itself. My Music Television education has been for nothing. This girl does not have gold teeth and a spray tan.

It takes some time but she eventually makes her way to the door, lifts her hand to knock then turns around, sits on the steps and rolls a cigarette.

Ophelia blows a smoke ring and it floats in the air. Like a halo, it hovers above her head for just a moment before it disappears.

I open the door. "Welcome to the Alexander residence. You're late."

"I missed the bus." She doesn't look back. "Nice place. In an old-money kind of way. I always wanted to see where Jane grew up."

Her voice is raspy, like her mother's, always on the verge of some kind of illness. Ophelia stubs out her cigarette, comes inside and sets down her plastic grocery bag. She is a pierced wreck of a thing with anarchist eyes, constantly pulling on her sleeves to hide her tattoos.

"So, this is the asylum. Is it true you made Jane take cold showers?"

"Cold showers are reformative. More so than lying on a couch, complaining to a stranger."

"Right." Ophelia twirls the ring in her nose.

I have seen young people with rings in the sides of their noses but hers is in the middle, as with a bull. Ophelia removes her boots, which takes several minutes as they are laced up to her knees. When they come off, she has tattoos on her feet and one toenail is wearing an earring.

"Did you come here to write your manifesto?"

"Relax, Judy, I wrote my manifesto ages ago."

"You may call me Judith in the house and Grandmother Alexander when we are out."

"Hey Jude, when was the last time you got laid?"

I think about asking her to make alternative arrangements for the summer but I know she will live on the streets with other hoodlums and they will sit on a street corner with a mangy flea-bitten dog with a sign around its neck: *Feed me. Woof!* They will have a cause they are fighting for but can't quite name. The rich keep getting richer (amen) or something like that. I can't be responsible for dogs wearing signs.

I show her to Janie's old room, which is decorated for a ten-year-old, Strawberry Shortcake style. Seeing her in it almost makes me laugh.

"I'd like to take a shower. I feel gross from the bus," she says and starts scratching her arms.

"Yes, I'm sure you do." I consider that she may be a bed bug carrier.

She opens her plastic bag, filled only with food.

"I will feed you."

"Jane says you don't even know what junk food is. I couldn't take chances."

I wonder what I will do with a girl who thinks packing Cheetos is more important than a well-pressed blouse. But Janie likes to remind me she wouldn't be a heroin addict if I had given her a normal childhood. Keeping Ophelia is the least I can do.

"I'm going to prepare food. I'm sure you have something more appropriate to change into for dinner?"

"Actually, my Vera Wang is at the cleaners."


After her shower, Ophelia thunders around upstairs. I figure she is planning to loot the place, smash and grab my figurines, but when I check she is wandering aimlessly, naked except for a hand towel wrapped around her head—the kind that are meant to be looked at, not used. She holds a small computer in front of her like it's guiding her from room to room.

"Do you seriously not have WiFi?"

I can't help but stare at her pubic hair, which has been sculpted into the shape of a small dagger.

"How am I supposed to watch porn? I just got here and already feel like dry humping the sofa."

"Pornography is immoral and illegal."

"Only if it involves children."

I know what the Internet is but hate calling people and asking for help. There is always some foetus at the end of the line trying to make me feel inferior. I don't know what an email address is or why I would need one when I have a postman (Henry) and a mailbox. I confess this to Ophelia. While playing with her nose ring, she says she will have it set up for me in a day. "Trust me. You need email."

She reviews the benefits of this messaging system. I find this helpful and look forward to email. Even the bridge ladies are sending evites now. I had a husband once and it is in moments like this I miss him. He would have taken care of WiFi for me. He would have helped me with Janie.

"Are you naked because you have no clothes?" I ask.

Ophelia nods. "I don't want to put my clothes back on until they're washed."

I open her mother's old closet. She grabs a few dresses wrapped in plastic to contain their ruffles. "I can't imagine Jane wearing these things."

"She didn't really. Take what you want but you have to give me those."

Ophelia reluctantly hands over her black tights and sweater.

"It's for the best."

She finds a few sweaters as well, which I realize are her gifts from last Christmas.

"These are wicked ugly," she says.

"True dat," I say and she makes me promise never to say it again. Ever.

At dinner, Ophelia comes to the table wearing one of her mother's dresses with an ugly Christmas sweater over top. It has skis and poles crisscrossed in the front and back. She has hacked one of the dresses to the knee. Her hair is pulled back, revealing four colours not found in nature. She is a vandalized version of Janie when she was younger.

Ophelia notices her own clothes burning in the fireplace behind us but says nothing. Instead, she goes on about all the things I can do on the Internet. "You can even order sex toys."

"That won't be necessary but thank you for your assistance with WiFi," I say.

Ophelia spits out an artichoke heart and wipes it on the side of her plate, somehow reminding me of wiping dog doo off the bottom of one's shoe.

"Don't thank me. I'll die if I'm not connected." She has a cellular phone and though it doesn't seem to work, she keeps mashing the keys.

The next morning, Janie calls.

"Getting well isn't going well."

"That's not a greeting, Janie."

As she speaks, I imagine her grey and shaking in a corner somewhere, perhaps in a cell that smells of urine and bleach. I imagine her skeletal hand gripping the phone while the other picks at a wrist full of scabs. If Teddy had been a heroin addict, I imagine he would have been more dignified. He would have checked into one of those celebrity rehab places where they have spa services and good linen. Though his hands might shake, at least his cuticles would be pushed back.

"Did she make it okay?" Janie asks.

In the other room, Ophelia is rooting around in a bag of potato chips.

"Yes, she's here. Does she ever eat real food?"

"I make sure she gets three squares a day."

"Is there a reason for your call, Janie?" Instinctively, I want to find and clutch my purse.

A shopping cart clatters by, mixing with the noise in the background. She isn't in rehab; she is on a street corner somewhere.

"I need money."

"I have nothing to give you, Janie. You remind me of that all the time."


A few days later, when the WiFi man comes, Ophelia follows him around. I do not like strangers entering my home. I always feel they will come back and rape me once they figure out I live alone. Some young men have a thing for the elderly. Apparently it's a trend, although they don't have exact numbers. I had a husband once. He took care of scaring off rapists.

The service man, a boy really, has no interest in taking stock of the things in my home. He does not appear to have a thing for old ladies; he has a thing for Ophelia's legs, which are long and have python tattoos slithering up the inner thighs. Despite this, they are nice legs. No marbling, as my butcher would say. If she were hosed off and given a decent haircut, even I could see potential. They stand around the front door and talk. Before he leaves, he gives her his number. When the door closes, she rumples it up and throws it in the fireplace.

"As if," she says, smiling. As if we were co-conspirators. As if we were on the same team.

"As if," I say.

When my computer is set up, Ophelia sits down and shows me how to pick an email address and set my password. I type *duckie*. It is rejected.

"It has to be eight characters, including one capital and at least two numbers."

"Why? I'm just going to write it on a piece of paper and stick it right on the computer."

"Not my rules."

*Duckie12*

"Duckie?"

"My husband's pet name for me."

"I think you should try online dating," she says.

I have seen commercials advertising lonely local singles of all ages with varying commitment desires but I do not know how it really works. I met my husband at a wedding where he mistook me for a waitress. He said he married me because I was the only person who ever remembered to bring him milk. I still have no idea why I brought him milk when he ordered it. I should have explained I was the bride's second cousin on her mother's side and that I liked to wear black and white, which, I suppose, did make me look like the hired help. Instead I said, "I'll be right back."

Finding milk at a wedding is not easy but I did find cream.

"Everyone forgets the milk. But not you my little duck." He asked if we could meet when I finished my shift.

On our first date, my husband took me for a stroll around his vineyard. He exported wine. I loved saying this to people. Export. It sounded foreign to me then. Like a destination in itself. *"We're going to Export for the weekend."*

Throughout our marriage, we went for strolls around the vineyard and often took Teddy with us. We inspected our grapes. Janie rarely came, as she would often run away or pretend to run away but was really under her bed or beside the house hiding in the shrubbery. That's the thing with a large estate; sometimes it's impossible to find your children.

Each day, Ophelia shows me new things on the Internet. I dictate and she types. It takes some convincing but eventually, she takes me on a tour of thebiglovefactory.com. "Just to look."

The site is seizure inducing and confusing. "I prefer pet videos on YouTube."

"I seriously hope you're not doing the cat thing."

I shake my head.

"Aren't you lonely? I haven't been here that long and I'm already worried about eroding my clitoris."

"Must you say things like that?"

"It's the truth."

I suppose I am lonely. The gardener comes once a week but he never liked me much so I just spy on him to make sure he trims my bushes. I see my lawyer from time to time when I feel like changing my will—50/50; 47/53; 100/0. I do have friends but don't like going out in the evening and coming home to a dark house. I always suspect someone will be hiding in my curtains, ready to pounce on me. The thought of starting again, telling someone select stories from my past, feels tiring before I begin.

Ophelia says we won't fill out my profile with completely accurate information and, to start, we don't have to include a photo. It is common to do this at first and will make me less nervous. "Until you learn how to filter the douche-lords from the real men."

In the meantime, she says we could order me a vibrator called *The Sure Thing*. It will be packaged inconspicuously and my Visa bill will read Luxury 5.0. No one will know.

"Honestly Ophelia. I am your Grand Mother!"


Janie checked herself into a clinic. I always know when she has because, instead of calling, she starts mailing cryptic notes.

*Did you run over Rupert on purpose? How is Ophelia? Can you send me money for the canteen?*

*Janie,*

*All future correspondence should be emailed and, yes, that dog had it coming. Ophelia is fine. I made her wash her hair. I suspect this is an annual event? I hope you are taking this getting-well business seriously.*

*Your Mother*

For several nights, I can't fall asleep. I realize I am mistaking insomnia for excitement. I want to check my big love factory profile and then a few minutes later, I want to check it again. I want to see if I have been propositioned by any worthy gentlemen.

Each morning, Ophelia helps me filter through my responses. I am disappointed by how few there are. I had always thought of myself as desirable. I had weathered well. A world of distinguished men was available to me. I just had to say the word. What I seem to be attracting are men from Iraq, Egypt and Belarus, all telling me how marriageable and beautiful I am when they have never even seen me.

*Can tell just by beautiful words so soft and poetic.*

It is ridiculous to contemplate these strange possibilities and yet I do. Could I be in a relationship with someone I've never seen? Could I move to a war zone? Would I be happy looking at the pyramids every day? How hard is it to learn Russian?

"You'll get more normal responses if you include a photo," Ophelia says. "It doesn't have to be your own. Which celebrity do you think you look most like?"

"Bette Davis."

Ophelia finds a photo of Bette Davis and makes it a bit grainy. Soon, I start getting more responses, which is quite exciting and takes a lot of my time to consider. I cancel bridge. We order takeout. I need to choose carefully. I wasn't aware how many douche-lords were looking for love.

*Mom, Do you remember when you made me do weigh-ins?*

*Honey, I was setting you up for a brighter future. Fat girls have fewer opportunities. As do short ones, but I wasn't trying to stretch you now, was I?*

*P.S. I hope you haven't fallen in with the wrong crowd at rehab.*


After filtering through my numerous propositions, I finally decide to communicate with a man named Roger OK who claims he is a duke and owns a castle just outside of Edinburgh. I could live in a castle though I've heard they're very draughty and often haunted.

*Dearest Roger OK,*

*Thank you for sending me a twinkle. As you must know, it is one of many twinkles I have received from around the world since joining the big love factory. But of all my potential suitors, I have chosen you! Please tell me more about your moat and plans to install alligators. Is that a joke? This seems primitive but I didn't realize there were still clansmen in your country.*

*Ms. Judith Alexander*

*P.S. Do you wear a kilt?*

After I hit send, I look at Roger OK's face for a long time. I had a particular image of what a duke from Scotland might look like, but Roger OK is more of a Wyatt Earp type. I find this disappointing though I can't help but wonder what it would be like to kiss a man with a handlebar moustache or to feel it zipping up and down other places. Of course, this may not be his real picture. He may look like someone else altogether.

To cast a wider net, I also communicate with a few lonely local singles. UplusMe seems like a nice fellow. I send him a twinkle. Ophelia says I should try and arrange a date with one of them soon. "Don't make a big deal about it. It will only make you nervous."

I ask her if dating rules have changed much.

"Pubic hair has gone out of style," she says.

"All of it?"

"Depends on the date."

I ask her about her dagger and if she does it herself.

"Yes, but I've since given myself a Brazilian." She pauses. "Baldie," she says and makes a circle motion around her crotch. "Don't be surprised if one of these guys asks you how you trim your hedges."

She tells me even grannies aren't allowed to wear granny panties anymore. They must wear something called bootie shorts. I think about my adult diapers and wonder if my date would be sympathetic if I told him incontinence affects one out of every three women.

"Do you have a boyfriend?" I ask.

She shows me a picture of a boy with blue hair who is wearing eyeliner. He has earrings through his eyebrows and one in his cheek.

"Are you in contact?" If I were her, I can only imagine being filled with glee to have this blue-haired person out of my life, but she looks distressed by the question.

She waves her phone. "Sort of. We text but we're taking a break while I'm here."

"What does that mean?"

"Mostly that he's seeing other people. I would too but your gardener's not my type."

Ophelia reviews a few more dating rules. "Don't get roofied," she advises.

We pick a code word: duckie. She will call at a certain time. If I am in trouble but can't say anything obvious, *duckie* will save me.


Over the next few weeks, I stay up late into the night and send notes to Roger OK. When he takes more than five minutes to respond, I get worried. I worry I may be falling in love with him. Ophelia calls them e-crushes and tells me not to get too caught up in things.

Still, I start to clearly see myself living in a castle. Cozying up around his fireplace while reclining on a bear skin rug. Hunting rabbits on weekends. Before I get too far ahead of myself, Ophelia suggests we meet.

Roger OK promptly asks if I will wire him money for his plane ticket as his country is in a recession and he is temporarily having a hard time making his castle payments. Ophelia barely takes a breath before she is clacking away on the keyboard.

*Goodbye, Roger OK. Duke of the Douche-Lords.*

I decide to meet a local gentleman before my imagination runs amok again. Ophelia helps me find something to wear. As she sifts through my closet, she says, "You should pleasure yourself with *The Sure Thing* before you leave."

I hang up the dress I'm looking at and move deeper into the closet.

"You either bought *The Sure Thing* or keep a weed wacker in your bedroom."

*The Sure Thing* is very noisy. Of course there was no mention of this in the advertisement. It does however, do everything else it promises.

She smiles. "Don't you have jeans or something black?" She pulls out a lime green jacket and matching skirt.

"That suit highlights my vibrant personality. Brocade never goes out of style."

"It burns my retinas. Don't you have anything less matchy-matchy? You're not Jackie O."

She makes colour coordination sound like a disease and under no circumstances am I allowed to wear my mink stole.

I drive to the lounge and circle around in the car for a while. Sometimes, when the temperature and breeze are just right, it lifts the scent of my husband's cologne buried deep in the car seats. I press my hand into the cushions. For a moment, he is beside me again. There is no need for ridiculousness. Drinks with strangers.

I do wonder if he would want me to move on. Of course, it is an impossible question. Everyone says yes, but I'm not so sure.

I park and go inside, take a seat in the corner and order a Shirley Temple.

"I'm Bette Davis ordering a Shirley Temple," I tell the waitress, who nods and asks if I would like peanuts.

After about an hour, the manager comes over with a bottle of pink wine.

"This is from the Eagle Has Landed. He called to say he's sorry but he can't make it."

"Ever?"

"Didn't say."

The harder I try to stay composed, the more my chin starts to warble. I cry into my peanut bowl until the manager asks me to leave.

"Just a moment," I say, dabbing at my eyes with my Hermès handkerchief.

I expect him to walk me to my car, but he shakes his head. "Lady, you're bad for business. You cry ugly."

I had always thought I was a lovely crier. Dainty. Mysterious. I go to the washroom and see that I do in fact cry ugly. If I once thought there was a line-up of princes and dukes circling the gates, this is behind me now. There will be no one to tell select stories from my past.


When I come home, Ophelia is in my bath robe and has her hand stuck in a bag of Doritos. I let my coat fall to the floor and tell her the Eagle Has Landed was a no show.

"We'll try again," she says.

"I don't think I will try again."

"You say that now."

We walk upstairs and she runs a bath for me. *The Sure Thing* is waterproof. When I get out, I ask her to help me take down my profile, which proves much harder than we imagined. I end up writing many emails to the big love factory, in which I tell them I am not who I said or thought I was. But the fact that I am an easygoing, fun-loving Taurus who loves her children and long walks on the beach with her shih tzu stays right there in the *elderly and still looking for big love* category.


For the last week of Ophelia's stay, we watch a lot of TV in my bed, which is something she likes to do and I have grown fond of as well. I have never done this before and will likely stop when she leaves, but I find myself doing things that will make her want to stay here again or at least keep in touch.

Janie calls. There are sirens in the background, which I find oddly comforting.

"Everyone makes mistakes, Janie." Someone shuffles by. A dog barks. "It's easy to let the wrong people into your life. One minute, they're promising you a castle, the next you're crying into a peanut bowl. I got lucky. The right man asked me to bring him a glass of milk."

"Please put my mother back on the phone."

Ophelia climbs into bed with me and puts a bag of chips between us. She has taken another of her mother's debutante dresses, ripped the sleeves off and cut it to mid-thigh. The hem is jagged as if she has been attacked by a pit bull. She has an ugly Christmas sweater tied around her waist. I put the call on speakerphone.

"Hi, Mom," Ophelia says.

We find a movie on TV. It's part-way through and is the annoying foreign kind you have to read, but it takes place in Paris and is lovely to watch. From time to time, through the phone, we hear someone shouting or a car door slam. Ophelia reads the subtitles for her mother and describes the scenes. Endless cobblestone. Small cars on roundabouts.

"What's happening now?" Janie asks.

Janie at a payphone with a million tiny holes punched up and down her arms, underneath her fingernails, the tops of her feet. *They just took a seat at a café.* Janie with no teeth. *The Ferris wheel spins.* I would buy her teeth. If she would just come home. *Grandma would like Parisian men.* But Janie will never come home. *These people seriously need to talk less with their hands.* She will never again have teeth. Her skin will always be picked over, sieve-like.

This is the closest we will ever come to being together and trying to enjoy something at the exact same time. The closest we will ever come to enjoying a street café in Paris. As Janie starts to argue with someone, the chances of another moment like this slip—75%...50%.

"Lady, you've been flapping your trap for over an hour."

25%. It is a man's voice. Gruff and hard but I want Janie to fight so she can stay here with us in Paris. 15%.

Onscreen, our characters get up and walk hand-in-hand down the Champs-Élysées. 0%. Gone. Although I know I am speaking to a phone receiver left dangling, I tell my daughter, "Pay attention, Janie. The best part is still coming."

# THE END OF THE WORLD (NOW POSTPONED)

Jerome takes his seat—second row, behind the one reserved for mothers with infants. There is already a mother and infant onboard. Jerome wonders what it would be like to get pushed around in a stroller. Babies have it made. He could look around and point at things. *What dat?* No one has ever accused a baby of asking a stupid question.

Jerome might hang out of a stroller and at thirty-five, guesses he is a bit too old. Doesn't matter. He doesn't have anyone to push him around anyway. This is not something to be sad about.

Jerome nods to the bus driver who always waits for him to take his seat before he drives off. Jerome looks at his watch. It will seem much longer but it will only be approximately three minutes and twenty-two seconds until Emily gets on the bus and does not sit beside him. Until she gets on the bus and he does not tell her about his plans for their future, which include, among other things, his starting a business—a horse-drawn café.

He carries a carnation for her lapel, just in case she talks to him and agrees to a date. He does not think she will talk to him because about a month ago, he called her seeing eye dog, Bart, an asshole. Instead of guiding her, which is Bart's job (it even says so on his vest), he was eating sandwich crusts off the ground and led Emily into a pole.

Jerome came running to her rescue but the dog growled at him and Emily said Bart was not an asshole, he was just hungry after a long day of working selflessly to guide her. As she said this, the pole was still vibrating and she was rubbing her forehead. When the dog was finished eating they moved along. Jerome was worried for her, so he followed until Bart turned around and would not stop growling.

"I'm fine. Leave me alone," Emily said as Bart led her toward the next restaurant.

Jerome left her alone. She was going to be his life partner but he didn't really know her. They rode the same bus sometimes, which might not sound like much, but this is how people meet. His own parents met when his mother was working in a library and helped his father find a book about fire ants.

On the bus, Jerome puts his thermal lunch pack on the seat beside him. It keeps hot things hot and cold things cold for up to four hours. He uses two compartments to transport his lunch and one to transport his chinchilla, Portia. Chinchillas make good pets because they are soft and fit neatly into Tupperware. Jerome used to let her ride on his shoulder but her enormous ears and frequent need for dust baths scared people. At first, he thought she could be trained to do tricks. He was wrong. Chinchillas are for companion purposes only.

More passengers get onboard. They see his thermal lunch pack wiggling on the seat and move on. If they stop near him, he nudges it a bit farther—toward the edge but not quite. He is not unfriendly. He is the kind of person people like to confess things to and he has grown tired of collecting secrets.

Jerome watches leaves fall and thinks of winter. Thinks of all the things he will have to do to prepare. Nothing. He lives in an apartment. He looks at his watch. One minute and thirteen seconds. He adjusts his plaid bowtie, which he hopes will match what Emily is wearing. She used to honour a Monday through Friday wardrobe system. Now, she dresses willy-nilly.

He watches the people on the bus read. The covers of some books are hidden. They crinkle newspapers. They sleep. They drink coffee out of travel mugs. They spill. They cough. They don't always cover their mouths. Some use the crook of their elbows like they are supposed to. Some slather on antibacterial gel. They sniffle. They put used tissue up their sleeves. Some stand. They rock. They sway. They turn the corner. Emily waits.

She has on the thick shoes today. Not the other ones. She has on the long dress, the green one that reminds him of a tablecloth. Gingham. He has a gingham bowtie but it is at home. The gingham dress is the one that trips her when she walks up the stairs. He would like to have her dress hemmed for her—$7.99 at Tip Top. He knows it would be very difficult to ask her for her dress. So he doesn't. He keeps his trap shut, like his father often tells him to. The good deed of hemming goes undone. Still, he worries.

She carries her lunch in a plastic grocery bag. The tines of her fork poke through. This is a hazard. He wants to tell her about thermal lunch packs. That he likes her other shoes better. The ones with the thick rubbery soles and fake leopard fur around the ankles. She walks past him. It is still dark outside but she wears her heavy sunglasses. He moves his thermal lunch pack too late, feels Portia grow restless.

The man with pointy elbows picks up Jerome's thermal lunch pack and sits down beside him.

"What's inside?" the man asks.

Jerome clutches it to his chest. "It's classified."

The man tells Jerome what is inside his lunch bag. He also keeps power bars in his desk—like a chocolate bar, but full of vitamins and minerals he does not get otherwise. The man tells Jerome he has a fear of having a brain aneurism right before he is about to retire. Any other time would be fine.

For the rest of the ride, Jerome reads over the man's shoulder. He has no choice. He doesn't even like science fiction. Apparently the aliens are coming. Often, you can't tell them apart from real people. This makes Jerome nervous.

In the book, an alien is having a romance with a woman. Although she finds his rubbery, six-fingered hands strange, she does not realize he is an alien until he takes out his contact lenses and his eyes turn yellow and have red laser beams running through them.

"I don't like this part," Jerome says to the man.

"No problem." The man sticks a bookmark in the aliens, asks someone for the weather section of their newspaper. "We'll postpone the end of the world until tomorrow."

"Do you really think it will end?" Jerome asks.

"At some point, yes. Maybe not tomorrow."

Jerome feels time running out and wonders what he could do to impress Emily. With his horse-drawn café, he could make her foamy drinks and drive her around the city (no charge). He does not know if this is impressive. His father certainly did not think so.

When he gets up, he thinks about accidentally on purpose stepping on her foot. Instead, he bends down and sticks the carnation between her shoelaces. He rings the bell and gets off one stop too late.

At work, he puts Portia in his locker. He turns on a small reading light before he closes the door. He works in a factory that makes replicas of factories. He spends his days attaching tiny smoke stacks, assembling miniature forklifts and planting small evergreens.

He tells the cleaning lady about the aliens. She brings her radio over and they listen to CUFO 680, the station dedicated to interplanetary affairs.

*You're on the air.*

*I was on my way to be abducted when the greys stopped to have a little round table discussion. All of a sudden, they dropped me. Is this common?*

*Somewhat. For whatever reason, the greys lose interest in certain people. They probably had what they needed from you.*

*I liked being useful.*

*Sometimes things don't work out as we'd hoped. Next caller.*

Jerome gets on the bus.

"Morning."

"Morning."

He would like to say something more, something more than "morning." He would like to show the driver Portia, thinks he would appreciate her but he's not sure. He's been wrong before.

"Everything okay?" the driver asks.

"I have to get my picture taken for my bus pass now."

"Anything to make life a bit more difficult."

Jerome nods.

"Maybe you should take a seat before I pull away?"

Jerome nods again and takes his seat. The driver told him a secret once. When he's off duty, his hobby is running red lights.

Jerome looks at his watch. It will seem much longer but it will only be three minutes and twenty-two seconds until Emily gets on the bus and does not sit beside him. His plans for their future have grown more elaborate. He is wearing his gingham bowtie today and hopes they will match.

Jerome puts his thermal lunch pack down. It keeps hot things hot and cold things cold for up to four hours. He places it on the seat beside him. If they stop near him, he nudges it a bit farther—toward the edge, but not quite.

Snow drifts across the roads. The banks are high and he feels like they are driving through a tunnel. He has the strange feeling the bus is not moving but the scenery is. There is no other traffic.

The people on the bus mutter complaints about the wind and cold. Wonder why they live here. Coffee steams from their cups. Their zippers are frozen shut. Tiny icicles have formed on their eyelashes. They talk about their office Christmas party. Jerome tries to tune them out—hums *Jingle Bell Rock*.

At the party, someone stood on their tippy toes and photocopied their private parts. *What a bright time.* This person emailed an image of their squashed cherries. Re: Have a Berry Merry Christmas. This person got fired. *It's the right time.* They are sombre while reporting this event. *To rock the night away.* After a moment of being sombre, someone asks if the fired person Photoshopped the image before he sent it? Or do they really look like that?

*Jingle bell time.* Jerome wonders how this cherry photocopying person will buy presents for his family. *Giddy-up jingle horse, pick up your feet.* He is glad when they stop talking about their office.

Although it is still dark, Emily has on the sunglasses, which make her look like a Terminator. She does not have a bus pass. He wants to tell her she could save $15.95 each month by buying one. Her hand misses the box and her coins spill down the aisle. Bart sniffs the coins. Different hands, including his, reach toward her to return the coins. His hand is lost among many hands. She says thank you, but he knows it is universal. Knows he will not be receiving a thank you card in the mail. She gives the coins to the driver who puts them in the box.

She sits down in front of him—in the seat reserved for mothers with infants. He wants to tell her she is not a mother with an infant. Wants to warn her of the perils of expecting mothers (i.e., they are often very grouchy and don't like whiners). He wants to tell her about the revamped business plan for his horse-drawn café. He has a box of chocolates for her. He has only eaten one.

The man with the pointy elbows gets on the bus. He sits down beside Jerome and opens his novel. He holds it between them. They are almost finished. It seems very unlikely that aliens will take over the world. Jerome is relieved. The man tells him this is just one book in a series of eight, so there's always time for the world to end.

Jerome rings the bell for his stop. He cannot look up when he passes her. She is wearing the other shoes. He smiles, then notices they have almost no tread, worries she might have a slip and fall.

"Merry Christmas." He gives the driver the chocolates. He has only eaten two.

At work it is just Jerome and the cleaning lady. They let Portia run around one of the little steel mills. They look through the paper together and she helps him decide which movie to see on Christmas day.

*You're listening to CUFO 680. Next caller.*

*Why do primitive aliens have such bad breath? If they're so smart and come here to probe my brains, why can't they learn to brush their teeth or zap their mouths with special lasers or something? I can't stand when they hover over me and all I can smell is dirty socks and wet dog.*

*Maybe they're trying to distract you from what they're doing. Get you thinking about Crest whitening strips instead of the enema. That's not so stupid, now is it? Next caller.*

Jerome gets on the bus.

"Morning."

"Morning."

He likes the sprouting grass and melting snow banks. Portia wiggles. The bus sprays people with mud and water. Spring showers. They are waking up. They are yawning and stretching their arms. They are blowing the stink off. They are airing out. They recount a long cold winter like it was a story they heard a long time ago—a winter lived by someone else. A pioneer or a fur trader. They have cottages they had almost forgotten about, tucked behind pine trees and cobwebs. They talk about lakes and fishing. Taking the first dip.

Jerome too would like to take a dip. He would like to be invited to these cottages where they grill salmon on cedar planks. Where they cut meat and vegetables into cubes and roast them on a stick. Where they drink beer and shoot the shit. But he has his own spring rituals. A new thermal lunch pack, for one. For another, his own family will be coming to visit him soon. They will survey his apartment, search for signs he is integrating well.

His sister will sip her tea and ask him to come for a visit. Jerome knows she will make him eat flax for breakfast. She will tell him he can get to know his nephews better. He remembers how they painted his fingernails the last time he was getting to know them better. Pink with sparkles. *You're so pretty, Jerome.* He wore gloves until the cleaning lady took the polish off for him.

When his family comes, he will look for strange markings on his sister's neck. Possibly in the shape of triangles. He will hide Portia. His mother will roam around opening and slamming doors, trying to figure out what stinks. She will ask him if he has learned anything new or met any new friends. He will tell her about the man on the bus and the aliens. Especially the aliens. How they may or may not be coming. How if you wake up in your backyard nude, you have probably been abducted. How the very last thing aliens do when you get abducted is give you a guided tour of their spaceship and a pamphlet to peruse later, at your leisure.

"Stop this flying saucer nonsense!" his mother will say.

He will not tell his mother about the girl with the shoes, both pairs. How if she had a secret to tell him, he would keep it sealed in his thermal lunch pack. The hot or cold side, whichever she prefers. He will not tell his mother about the girl because it is difficult to talk about her. Sometimes she is a blink of flashing light, then gone.

His father is a bug man at the university. He likes to be asked questions about chestnut weevils and turnip moths. Jerome does not like his father talking about killing jars or having to grip bugs a certain way so he doesn't damage the specimen. He does not like the way his father stands there with his eyes closed while pinching his thumb and index finger together.

They will leave. Jerome will relax. He will yell out his window, warn all bugs to run for their lives. He will release Portia. They will inhale spring. She will take a dust bath. He will no longer wish to be at the lake with the people from the bus, to spend time with their families. He has his own and they are a handful.

The bus turns the corner. She stands at the bus stop, holding a white cane. No Bart today. She has a cane trainer with her. She whacks her cane around and climbs up the steps.

"Use it to help you with distance," the cane trainer says.

He wants to tell the cane trainer she always trips on the steps, that there is nothing wrong with her. Especially when she has the gingham dress on, which she does. The cane trainer should help her whack her way to Tip Top where she could get her dress hemmed. Jerome could accompany them.

A man grabs her by the elbow. She has what his nephews would call a flip out. The elbow-grabbing person apologizes. The cane trainer tells the man to always offer your arm before grabbing hold. Jerome takes note.

She whacks her way to her seat. Even with her cane trainer, she sits on top of a new mother with a baby on her lap. The baby cries. The mother says it is okay but everyone knows it is never okay to crush babies.

She hangs her head. Hands reach out and offer her tissues. His hand is lost in a sea of hands. His tissue has aloe in it. It will be softer and more comforting than the rest of the tissues—especially the one he suspects has been gently used. He saw it come out of someone's sleeve. He convinces himself it was merely crumpled. She is in no real danger of getting a virus.

The man with the pointy elbows opens a new book. In this one, the aliens aren't in disguise. They don't try to be friendly first. They abduct people, probe them, set them free. Often these people don't remember why they were missing and their wives get angry that they are late for dinner and accuse them of having an affair. It gets complicated.

At work, they are fundraising. They send Jerome to the mall with a collection box around his neck. His boss tells him that when people see a person like Jerome, they dig a little deeper.

There is no CUFO today.


Jerome gets on the bus. There is a new driver.

"Morning."

The new driver grunts then accelerates before Jerome is off the stairs. He struggles to get his pass out. His new picture is handsome. The lady at the grocery store said so. The new driver does not look at Jerome's bus pass. Will not know how handsome he is. Jerome would like to see his eyes. Check them for red laser beams. The metal bar bangs Jerome's hip before he can sit down.

Most of them do not get on the bus. Most of them are at their cottages winging around the lake in dinghies. Most of them are buying worms by the pailful from a seven-year-old saving for a telescope. They pay full price for his worms. Ask him about his digging routines.

They are inspired. They too want to be stargazers, to see a bright light in the sky that makes them forget the smell of the bus, about waiting for it to come and the feeling of dread when it actually does.

The man with the pointy elbows is not at the lake. He plans to spend his summer with aliens. Even though there are empty seats, he sits beside Jerome.

"Hot enough for ya?"

Jerome nods, notices the wet marks beneath the man's underarms. He wants to recommend a particular deodorant but doesn't. This particular deodorant does not contain aluminum and will not make you forget things when you grow up to be old.

The man opens their book. They are well into a new one in which the aliens have landed and don't bother trying to disguise themselves. They are grey and proud of it, though sometimes they morph into a kind of fog so when people are at home watching TV, they should know they are about to be invaded when green mist starts to appear under the door. By the next page, the greys will be along with their deep sinkhole eyes.

Jerome's bus makes a sudden stop. A green light flashes. A strange whirring noise seems to come from above. He prepares to partake in the making of crop circles. When he looks again, it is just a stuck traffic light and no one knows whose turn it is so everyone is honking.

She waits at her stop with a new dog. It guides her up the steps. Jerome notices her shoelace is undone. The dog is likely a good dog but it can't tie shoes. Jerome wants to tell her about Velcro.

While the bus is still stopped, Jerome kneels down, makes two rabbit ears, crosses them and pulls gently. He wonders if she would like to touch his face. He saw this in a movie once. When he is about to give her the details of his horse-drawn café, the driver accelerates quickly. Jerome falls, puts his palm out to stop himself and crushes his thermal lunch pack. It's not good. Hot. Cold. Miscellaneous.

They help him up. Wonder why he is allowed to be alone. Without supervision. They feel bad for thinking these things. As they dust him off, they wonder where he works. They give him back his lunch. Ask him if he is okay but do not know what they will do if he says no. When he does not answer they are relieved. They do not want to be late for work.

Jerome looks at her dog scratching his ear. He rings for his stop, which has long passed. She stares straight ahead. Itches her foot. Then pets her dog. At the factory, Jerome's manager asks him where he has been.

"I got a little lost," Jerome says.

"I'll make you a good map. That should help."

Jerome sits down and looks inside his thermal lunch pack. Portia has an injured leg but is otherwise okay. He will take her to the vet even though this is expensive and he does not have a credit card. (Which is not his fault. He has applied many times.)

The cleaning lady applies a salve to Portia's leg and helps him make a tourniquet.

*You're listening to CUFO. You're on the air.*

*Can abductions be arranged?*

*The greys know exactly who they want. There's not a waiting list.*

*Well, if you know of any aliens who do pick-ups, I'm available. I'll give you my address.*

*Trust me. If you're of use to them, they'll find you. If you have nothing to offer, they'll just keep going. Next caller.*

Jerome hangs up the phone, thinks about the relief of being sucked onboard a whirling disk, hovering over the planet while having his mind squeegied by an alien. He understands now why people believe in these waxy-fingered creatures: to forget, to take a chunk of time, throw it away, watch it rain fireworks in a galaxy far far away and return to earth in time for dinner.

# HYBRID VIGOUR

After our phone call, I try to imagine what my father might look like. In my mother's wedding photo his face is a burn hole I would often stick the tip of my pinkie through. Sometimes I would draw features on my little finger. One winking eye. Puckered lips.

"You'll know me when you see me," he said.

"No, I don't think so."

Then he hung up.

If he had stayed on the phone a little longer I would have told him I needed to talk to him because I'm failing journalism school and have to write a story that will make my instructor cry out of something other than frustration. She actually sighed when she flung my last assignment—an exposé on doggie DNA testing: *Is There a Great Dane Lurking in Your Chihuahua?*—across her desk.

"This was supposed to be a critical piece. You made your article on *Purebred Puppies? Inc.* sound like a product endorsement," she said.

"I stressed the tests are only partially accurate. Pet parents everywhere will be alarmed."

"Pet parents are one thing. You can't fake an interview with a dog and expect me to take you seriously."

I did include a few quotes from a dog that had been wrongly assessed as a beagle, only to find out later he was really a Pomeranian. This is what my instructor calls a lack of credibility. Instead of a rewrite, she assigned me a new story.

"Give me something with real personality." Between words, she snapped her jaws like a mousing terrier. "And it better be bloggable."

A red F was gouged into the paper.

I stick it on my fridge beside the overdue credit card bill. In addition to getting an excellent father-daughter reunion story, I intend to shake him down for eighteen years of child support: *Deadbeat Dad Pays Dues.*

Growing up, my mother didn't tell me much about my father. She didn't pollute me with stories about his illegitimate children littered around the globe. She didn't tell me he left us to become a crocodile wrangler or a yak breeder. In our house, we found it more convenient that he was made of mist and fog, morphing as we saw fit.

"Who left the butter out?"

"Dad."

"Who used all the hot water?"

"Your father. Damn that man."

We liked him crouching in the fridge, leaving only the branches from the grapes. We preferred him squatting in the breadbox, nibbling away, leaving only the crusts.

As I walk to the café where my father and I had arranged to meet, I take out my notepad and think about different ways to get him talking. I want to avoid awkward pauses—particularly at the money part. My journalism instructor always says to start with a lob question; be curious but not nosey, friendly but not overly. If he's a Harvard graduate, we'll talk about rowing and crew neck sweaters. If he's an investor, we'll talk about hedge funds. This will lead us straight to the child support issue. A natural segue my instructor calls it.

My father will say, "Yes, and it's so important that I repay you in today's dollars, plus interest." (Heart warming. Very bloggable.)

In front of me on the sidewalk, a group of men is just getting off work. They are taking off their jackets, swinging them over their shoulders, loosening their ties.

"Are you my father?" I ask.

They look back like scared sheep, then cross the street.

"Just checking!"

Not my best lob question, I'll admit.

At the café, I look through the window. There is only one customer. I go inside, order coffee and wonder if the barista is my dad. He looks a bit younger than me but I'm sure these things happen. You read about them all the time. I notice the scar on the inside of his hand, which is exactly like mine. *Scar Tissue: Old Wounds Reunite Estranged Father and Daughter.*

"Sugar and cream are that way," my dad says after I stare at him for what some might call an awkward amount of time.

I sip my coffee and watch the person sitting across from me—a hairy dude wearing a skirt and fishnets. Black leg hairs sprout through the holes. Could this be my she-dad? *Estranged Daughter Game for Hairy Truth.* I walk over and try to think of a friendly lob question about fishnets when he looks at me and says, "Shoo."

"I feel like we might be kindred spirits," I say. "We're both looking for something."

"Not looking for damn thing," he says, then walks out and takes his hairy fishnetted legs with him.

"I like your hosiery!"

I won't lie; I'm relieved. Along with the hope of finding my father, there is also fear. What if he's a nut job or a gym teacher? What if he is balding but grows what hair he does have into a long ponytail and talks endlessly about the original team of Greenpeace eco-warriors? What if, after all these years

I've given him a fabulous life as a magician, a mountain climber, a trapeze artist, and he turns out to be ordinary?

I look at my watch. I'm sure my fabulous father will be here any minute now. In the meantime, I order a veggie burger. When it arrives, I eat the sesame seeds off the bun first and count them (213 sesame seeds). I nibble the lettuce. I dice the tomato with the handle of my spoon and eat each piece slowly. With each bite of the patty, I try to identify flavours: flax, sweet potato, barley. Eating this veggie burger is serious business. I am an investigative journalist. When my analysis is finished and I am satisfied I have learned all I possibly can about my veggie burger, it is dark outside and the café is closing.

"I'm waiting for someone," I say, when the barista, my ex-father, asks me to leave.

"I don't think tonight's the night," he says and gestures toward the door.

On the way back to my apartment, dad-less, a man holds out his hand and asks for spare change.

"It's for the bus."

*Orphaned Girl Reunites with Homeless Father.* I give him a quarter. He looks at it. "Is that all you got?"

"It's more than I've got."

Growing up, I used to tell people my dad had a lot of money.

"Well, what does he *do*?"

"He's rich. It's a full-time job."

Sometimes my dad was a famous artist. Once when I was on a date, we walked past an enormous metal sculpture—the kind that looks like it's trying to strangle itself. I pointed and said, "My father made that."

My date (a bit of a dud) looked at me with shiny new interest. "I want to do my thesis on Arnold's work. I find his stuff so electrifying. Does it have the same effect on you?"

"Not really. It just makes me hungry." I rubbed my stomach and tried pulling him away but he refused.

"Can I meet him? I've heard he's very reclusive."

"Yes, few people have ever met him."

"What does he look like?"

I held up my pinkie. "Like this."

My date let go of my hand.

When I get home, I check my messages.

"Hey kiddo. Daddy here. Sorry, got tied up. Let's meet..."

The message keeps going, cutting in and out. But it is a fake kind of cutting in and out. Like he's pretending he's going through a tunnel but is just blowing into the phone and saying a bunch of random words: pumice, granite, bamboo, leotards.

My instructor says a good journalist doesn't get emotional. She remains impartial. She doesn't insert herself into the story. So I remain impartial and think about reasonable explanations for why he couldn't make it.

*Window Washer Dangles Overnight from Fiftieth Floor*

*Somali Pirates Strike Again!*

I look at my call display. His number is listed as unavailable. Figures. I think about other story possibilities. I could cover the children's festival. There will be pony rides, face painting and balloon tubes twisted into dachshunds. This has some personality but probably not enough to keep me from failing.

I call my mother and tell her about my search for daddy.

"Have I taught you nothing?" she asks. "An absent man is more useful." She starts complaining about my father and how he has dishes stacked to the ceiling, the lawn hasn't been mowed for weeks, he hasn't done laundry for years and is walking around with no underwear on as we speak.

"Junk in plain view. No wonder the neighbours never say hello."

With only a few days left to write my story, I decide to hire a detective. I consider her more of a fact checker, which most journalists need now anyway to enhance and verify the truth. First, I need to find someone willing to work for free until I get my eighteen years of child support (in today's dollars, plus interest). I spend all morning on the phone before I find someone who agrees.

When Samantha arrives, she is wearing an oversized trench coat and a detective hat. Although it's pulled over her face, she looks eight or nine years old and drinks coffee from a sippie cup.

"Youth and inexperience are not the same thing," she says.

She hands me her business card, which reads: *Samantha Taggert P.I. — Finding Crooks Since 1909.*

"Do you have credentials?"

"I did my detective training online."

I show her the photo of daddy.

"I'm not sure this will help."

I put my pinkie through the burn hole. "How about now?"

"I'm getting the picture. Tell me exactly what he said the last time you spoke." She whips out her notepad.

"He said he missed me."

"Touching. What did you say?"

"I said I've always wondered why I like blue cheese dressing so much. Did I inherit this or is there really something to this acquired taste thing?"

"Good question. Did the phone line sound crackly?"

"No."

"He's likely somewhere in North America."

"Seems like a broad search area."

I play Samantha the daddy message. She looks at the machine through a magnifying glass. "This guy's got issues."

Working with no money upfront, Samantha suggests I come along to speed things up.

"Plus you can drive. It's tough doing detective work on the bus."

This seems very bloggable so I agree.

On the way to my car, I keep tripping on Samantha's trench coat, which trails several feet behind her.

"Maybe you'd see more clues if you took off your hat?" I suggest.

"I'm incognito."

"Right."

When we get in my car, Samantha tells me it smells like fermenting meat, human grease and pine trees. She writes this down.

"The first thing we need to do is return to the crime scene," she says.

"It was really just a café where I mistook the barista and a crossdresser for daddy."

"Close enough."

At the café, Samantha goes around asking people, "Have you seen this man?" Then she grabs my hand and shows them my pinkie.

Soon, we are asked to leave.

"Don't give up hope," Samantha says. She tails a man and waves me along. "This is likely him."

"How can you be sure?"

She grabs my finger and then looks at the guy's head. "Don't question the way I work."

I follow along. The man is on the phone, talking loudly. He has a selfish laugh. (A good journalist has to be objective.) I decide he is a metrosexual, good looking (at least from behind), possibly wearing control-top pantyhose. His shoes look expensive. Clearly, he has cash. He'll insist on buying me birthday presents (retroactive): a diamond tennis bracelet for high school grad and matching earrings for college grad (pending and somewhat in jeopardy). I get in front of the metrosexual and say, "Welcome to my life. I knew you'd come."

He points to his phone and waves me away. Samantha whacks him with her notepad. "You're wearing too many patterns!" she says. Then she runs away and I follow.

"Your search methods are unorthodox," I say.

Samantha tells me she is going to accelerate the process, as per lesson number seven of her online training course. When we get back to the car and drive around, she sticks her head out the window. To every man we pass, she yells, "Are you my daddy?"

"Was this really part of your training?" I ask.

"It's called the direct approach. Some things can't be taught."

As we drive around, it seems like the world is made only of men who run away or turn the corner just as I get close. In each one, there is a tiny pinkie-like possibility. My dad is everywhere and nowhere, everyone and no one.

"Do you have specific memories of daddy that might be helpful?" Samantha asks.

"He often ate my homework, never took out the garbage and was really the one who sprayed graffiti on our neighbour's garage."

"That'll be tough to fact check." Samantha reviews her notes. "But you're my first almost-paying customer. I won't let you down. He's out there somewhere."

We drive around looking for daddy until it is dark and the streets are deserted. Until it feels like the only people left in this city are me and Samantha.


The next day, Samantha comes over with a stack of papers. Using my parents' wedding photo, she made wanted posters. "There's an administrative fee for this but I'll cut you a deal if you help me put them up."

"I don't have five hundred dollars for a reward."

"Fine." She leaves in a huff.

Later that day, I go for a walk and see the posters of a faceless man every-where, stapled to telephone poles and bus shelters, lapping overtop of all concert and community announcements. Lost dogs and cats don't stand a chance. For the next few days, people call me with details of their sightings.


When I am almost out of time to finish my assignment, Samantha shows up.

"I found daddy," she says.

"How can you be sure it's him?"

"I followed a lead and I do my detective work by the book."

"What lead?"

"Something only a detective would notice."

"What's he like?"

"More of a big toe than a pinkie."

"Will he talk to me?"

"No, but he will fill out a questionnaire."

This does not sound like good journalism but it's getting late and it's still a form of asking questions. If nothing else, I've learned the truth is negotiable.

*Thank you for taking part in the daddy survey. Please note all of your answers will be considered on the record.*

1. *Where do you live?* _____

2. *On a scale of one to ten, how would you rate the kind of first impression you make? (circle one)*

   *excellent     average     poor*

   *10  9  8  7  6  5  4  3  2  1*

3. *What do you do for a living?* _____

4. *Are you aware of your family's medical history?*

   ○ *yes*

   ○ *no*

   *If yes, please check all that apply:*

   ○ *cancer (all kinds)*

   ○ *diabetes (either kind)*

   ○ *leukemia*

   ○ *other (please specify)* _____

5. *Have you ever been incarcerated? If yes, please specify.*

   _____

6. *Do you have any regrets?* _____

*7. What is your income level (after tax)? Check one:*

   ○ *less than $15,000*

   ○ *$15,000–$29,999*

   ○ *$30,000–$49,999*

   ○ *$50,000–$74,999*

   ○ *$75,000 and over*

When Samantha brings back the survey, she demands payment.

"Things didn't quite work out as I had hoped," I say.

"I did the best I could with what I was given."

"Do you take Visa?"

"I'm a cash-only operation."

I arrange a payment plan, which she seems satisfied with. Before she leaves, she says, "Your dad said he loves you. That's not on the survey but he wanted me to let you know you turned out far above average."

*On Scale of One to Ten, Daughter Rates Reunion with Daddy off the Charts*

*When I approached my dad at the café, his back was toward me. I approached slowly, a lifetime of waiting about to end. I took out my notebook and jotted down his smells: pine trees, human grease. I was thinking more along the lines of Old Spice but sometimes, life surprises you.*

*"It's me," I said to the back of his head. "Don't turn around."*

*He laughed a selfish laugh but stayed put and said, "Okay, I understand. You say when."*

*I told him I had a few questions first. After he answered, I would decide if I wanted him to turn around.*

*"Shoot," he said and sipped his coffee.*

*My father, who is free of all major illnesses and has never spent time in prison, has worked for the majority of his life as a metal sculpture artist. Peri-*

*odically, he has had to live on the streets and beg for change. The last time he was down but not out, a kind crossdresser named Mosha helped him figure out his life's path.*

"Without Mosha, I don't know where I'd be."

*As a tribute, he made a sculpture out of fishnet stockings and hairy manne-quin legs.* "I tried selling it to MoMa but they didn't bite."

*I told my dad it was safe to slowly turn around.*

"Where have you been my whole life?" *he asked.*

"Turn back. That was a stupid thing to say."

*He turned back. We had an awkward pause. Then he told me about how he sailed around the African coast on a raft until he was abducted by Somali pirates. When they realized no country would pay a cent for his release, they let him go, but made him swim.*

"Any idea what you might like to do when you finish school?"

"Journalist or I'll probably make a good detective."

"That sounds real good."

*Although he had hardly won me over, I let him turn around. His face was badly burned, parts of it seemed erased. I tried not to stare.*

"Accident. I set myself on fire. Long story."

*A lifetime of waiting for my father to turn around and then it was over. I took a seat and ordered a quinoa salad. I let my dad go on for over an hour about what a great kid I had turned out to be. Who was I to argue? He told me he had no regrets about leaving.* "It's the best thing that could have happened to you." *Then he gave me a gift: diamond earrings and a matching tennis bracelet.*

*When it was time for him to catch his flight back to the undisclosed loca-tion he came from, he asked if I would cover the cheque. I realized the earrings and bracelet were likely diamonelle.*

"Ever since the Mosha tribute, I've had a hard time being taken seriously by the sculpting community."

*I paid the bill and we got up to leave.*

"It's not goodbye," *he said and got a little misty-eyed,* "it's I'll see you when I see you."

*He left the café, put his worn suit jacket over his shoulder, loosened his tie and crossed the street. Before he turned the corner, he looked back but seemed unable to focus on anything. I looked at the sun, shining for the first time that day. I stared for too long and started seeing bright spots. When I looked back at my father, there was a tiny flame where his face should have been. And then he was gone.*

Because the truth about my father seems a bit thin, I give my teacher what I consider a bonus story: an exclusive on the Mormon Church book sale. When I get my work back, my instructor pats my shoulder and says, "The way you work boggles my mind."

"I'd hate to be like everyone else," I say.

"No chance of that."

She walks me to her office door and pushes me out more gently than she ever has before. On my assignments, she wrote: *You have a zany outlook on alphabetical order and the value of old Encyclopedia Britannica. I would cry but you make me so tired. D-. The story about your father hangs together strangely but, if nothing else, it has personality. C+. (Don't bother with the blog. You should seriously consider a career with the federal government.)*

With no child support pending (income less than $15,000), I write the credit card company and thank them for their correspondence. I advise them to cancel my account, citing irreconcilable differences about the notions of time, money and the true meaning of the word minimum.

Several weeks later, I receive a letter from Samantha.

*I hope this hasn't arrived too late to be included in your story but a few weeks after the survey, I was able to get a cheek swab from daddy. I stole the kit from your counter. (Sorry, but it was the most detectivey I've ever felt even though, of course, theft goes against everything I learned in my online course.)*

*I guess my investigation is complete. I hope you find these results helpful. I have kept them sealed for confidentiality. (The most important lesson stressed in my online course.)*

*Sam*

*P.S. Can I use you for a reference on my website? Also, your last payment is overdue.*

I hold the unopened DNA results and keep holding it. When I graduate, it is a folded square in the palm of my hand. When I see my first article in print, I rub the envelope across it. It is in my pocket when a boy I could never marry gets down on one knee with a tiny box shaking between his fingers. When I move to a different city for a better job, it is a fuzzy wad of paper, fallen behind dresser drawers.

"This important?" the mover asks and hands it to me.

"Not anymore."

I look inside.

*Dear Samantha Taggert P.I.:*

*We had some trouble reading your sample; however, it appears your dog is most likely a beagle coonhound cross. Both breeds are loyal and love to hunt though they are both prone to long, fruitless searches and bouts of howling.*

*Congratulations on having a pet with enviable hybrid vigour. We wish you and your dog a long and happy life.*

*Purebred Puppies? Inc.*

They include a reasonable facsimile of what my dog might look. I hold my pinkie next to it. Though I try one last time to find one, there is no resemblance.

# STEP ON
# A CRACK

The first time Bella, our house lady, told me I was getting a stepmother, she made it sound like I was getting a puppy. I wasn't sure what to expect. Bedtime stories had filled my head with stepmothers' warty noses and unreasonable curfews, fat-assed women who clomped around in shoes their feet poured out of.

Then you blew through the door, all willowy and delicate. I watched you from behind the sofa. You were soft angles and cashmere. I liked your billfold, the way you drew money from it to give the doorman a tip. You knew his name.

I admired your hands, all the tiny bones visible beneath the skin, each finger ending with your flaming manicure. I had heard my father talk about women who never lifted a finger and knew you were one of them.

My father lifted off your shawl. Unwrapped you. Next to your grace, he looked lumpy and unsure. I hoped I would never get lumpy. I hoped when I grew up, I would look like you—that I would have hands like you. As he guided you down the long hallway, your high heels were surprisingly soft on the marble floor. Your shoes sculpted to your feet.

When we met, I was pretending to be a potted plant.

"Are you a rubber tree or a blooming hibiscus?" You grabbed my hand like it was a leaf.

"The blooming one."

"Do you need a lot of water and sunlight to grow?"

I nodded. You bent down and kissed my cheek. Your scent was one I welcomed but could not name.

"Enough now." My father led you away.

When you turned sideways, I thought you were made of cardboard. You wore gloves and smoked long cigarettes on our balcony. Your skin was so pale and thin, I swear I could see smoke go down your throat and plume inside your lungs.

I thought you were a movie star who had come to act out scenes with me. I insisted on a clapperboard for Christmas. Act One: Scene One. My father assured me you were not acting. I watched you carefully anyway, inspected your palms for script lines. As your things trickled into our home, I looked through them to make sure they weren't props. Then the boxes stopped coming and finally you were all there. Unpacked.

Act Two: Scene One. You took me to my first swimming lesson of the year. You did not care to go in the water but checked to make sure my bag was properly stocked with towels and water wings. You took me as far as the girls' locker room where I was intercepted by a real mother.

You sat on the viewing balcony. I waved and you raised a gloved hand. I often hid behind the bulkhead to see if you would dive in and save me if I were drowning. When you couldn't see me, you stood up and called to my instructor. I took this as a good sign. Act Two: Scene Two. My father assured me he would sue anyone who let me drown. I had nothing to worry about.

I started to spend a lot of time in your closet and often brought play dates there. It was like a trip to a foreign land. We draped ourselves in your scarves. Bartered for your jewels with counterfeit money.

My friend Harriet found your fur coats stored in what she called body bags. She laid the bags on the floor and unzipped them. She explained that you had definitely murdered coyotes, mink, possibly a cheetah and, worst of all, bunnies. She said her mother would have to spit on you the next time she saw you. No offense.

I told her about your excellent skills as a stepmother. How you would alert the authorities if you thought I were drowning.

Harriet took the white coat out of its bag and handed it to me. She tore the lining and we could see where the bunnies had been stitched together. Act Three: Scene One. Sixty-three bunnies.

Harriet wrapped the coat around her shoulders and hopped around with it trailing behind her. "I mourn you sixty-three bunnies. God bless."

She twitched her nose and petted the coat. Harriett had her own bunny, a gentle French Angora. "They were likely killed execution style."

When she was done hopping, we arranged the coats on the floor and drew chalk outlines around them. Then we took all of your clothes and threw them off the balcony. Who knew what had been killed in the making of your other garments and intimate apparel?

Final Scene. I watched empty versions of you float down thirty storeys to the sidewalk below. You came out to smoke a cigarette. I watched a storm brewing in your lungs. Lightning flash between your fingertips. Silently, we watched pieces of you lying on the ground.

I kept watching for you long after you blew away.

You told me the happiest part of your wedding was that your dress remained spotless. You tucked it into its box.

"Except the underside of the train. But that isn't a realistic expectation. Is it?"

"Most people said you had no business wearing white to begin with. I guess it all worked out."

In silence, you slid the box beneath the bed. I asked for my white gloves back.

"They were the *something borrowed* part of your outfit."

You gave them back, spotless; the tiny jewels on the sides brighter than before. You amazed me. I always meant to tell you that. You knew a million and one different ways to remove a stain. Ink (hairspray). Gum (peanut butter). Mud (shaving cream). Blood (ammonia and cold water). You considered pure whites your greatest accomplishment. You hated static cling and walked around the house shushing your aerosol can. You were always sneezing and stormed around the penthouse saying we harboured allergens just to spite you. You watched me swim. I think you found the smell of chlorine intoxicating.

You were forever folding laundry and ironing things: purses and shoes, leather coats. You said wrinkles deeply offended you. You accused Bella of being a kleptomaniac when you couldn't find your Braun steamer. I defended Bella, though I did like the word kleptomaniac. I told my father about kleptomania. He didn't lie. He said I shouldn't listen to you because you were neurotic. I liked this word too. I told my teachers they were neurotic. I told my swimming coach that a kleptomaniac stole my earplugs. A whole new world of illness opened up to me.

Sometimes on weekends, we would lie in bed together.

"Not too close," you said.

I think you liked me but feared my sticky fingers and unsterilized hands. You may have used the term *germ factory*. I inched closer. When you finished your drink, you put a little sword in your mouth and sucked off the olives. I wanted that sword. Imagined all the tiny things I could spear; coveted a weapon easy to conceal.

"How can you eat olives so early?" I asked.

"Doctor's orders."

While you slept, I looked through your medications. The different shapes and colours. Some engraved with initials like our silverware. Your medicine was custom made. You were a one-of-a-kind neurotic. When I shaved the edges, the pills fit neatly into my Pez dispenser. I wandered around the schoolyard offering classmates lithium and Prozac straight from Homer Simpson's mouth.

You picked me up from school; promised the principal and all concerned parents a stern talking-to was in my future.

"It's imminent," you said and grabbed my hand.

Outside, you leapt onto the hood of a car, walked over the roof and onto the trunk, then leapt onto the next one. "I used to be a gymnast," you said. You complained about convertibles, car alarms and people who didn't wash their vehicles. "My feet were clean."

Along Fifth Avenue, we wrote *I'm a pig* and *help! wash me!* in the dirt encrusted on car doors. At the end of the block, a police officer stopped us. I denied I knew you, which did not stop him from stuffing us in the back of his cruiser.

"I'm not intoxicated," you said. "My balance has somehow been compromised. That! is the real mystery here."

I asked to speak to my lawyer, but my father arrived instead.

"I'm here to pick up my daughter, the drug dealer, and my wife, the drunk vandal."

We were inmates. My father, the warden.


My father accompanied me to the hospital for neurotic people. While he talked with the doctors, I found your room. You looked so small in your bed. I checked underneath for monsters and clowns or worse, dust balls.

"All clear," I said.

You smiled. I told you I was there to save you from static cling, to make your whites whiter, your colours brighter.

I gave you a basket of your favourites: eucalyptus laundry detergent, lint rollers and a lingerie wash bag. I also brought champagne. With your bandaged wrists, you twisted the cork off under the covers.

"Long live the mighty car jumper," I said.

"Cheers, you little shit disturber."

You tilted your head back and your drink disappeared. You said you loved champagne. Even when it spilled, it never left a stain.

I had my first drink with you. Warm Dom Pérignon out of a paper cup.

When my father found us, he put me in a wheelchair and rolled me out. I didn't want to leave you there, all twisted in your off-white gown. I drew my tiny sword but my father just laughed. I shouted a tipsy goodbye and finally understood your language. The hostile way the world spun toward you.

When I got home, I ran to the park and grass-stained my knees. I spilled cranberry juice down my father's white shirts. I hung them back up and let the dripping colour set in. I imagined you coming home and saying *this will take forever to get out.*


He drove up in a new car and you were perched beside him, hands on the steering wheel. More doors and possibilities swung open.

"You get my puberty years," I said as you came into our home. "We've got a lot to pack in."

You tussled my hair in a way that told me I would be tolerated.

"I've been getting email about breast enlargements. These things aren't going to grow themselves."

You walked away.

"I need an advisor! Do I rub them with dandelion root or wild Mexican yam?"

You had this way of disappearing when I needed you most. I called the police. Filed a missing persons. Dusted for fingerprints. Installed a nanny cam.

I had questions I needed to ask a mother: What about this period thing? I don't buy that I'll be doing cartwheels on the beach in a white bathing suit.

You left me a note.

*Google it.*

I hoped to see you at one of my events but you wrote letters of regret. A whole year's worth in advance.

*I regret to inform you I will not be attending the school musical. I hear you make a marvellous Annie. Break a leg.*

*I regret to inform you I will not be attending your piano recital. Break a finger.*

*I regret to inform you I will not be able to attend your swim meet as I find the odour of chlorine stifling. Break a fin.*

I tried to recall your face and couldn't. When you passed by mirrors I never saw a reflection. Just smoke. I thought it was because I was too short to see that high, so I grabbed a chair and followed you around. By the time I got to the mirror and climbed up? Nothing. I put mirrors in front of your face, then when I looked, I only saw myself.

You were so plain. I thought you must be the nanny. But you were his practical choice. His Chevy. You had underwear lines and sensible ideas. We would eat at the same times each day. Do my homework together. We would communicate.

We joined a support group and sat around in a love circle. We squeezed each other's hands. All stepdaughters wore black hoodies and broke the circle in order to bite their nails to the quick.

When it was my turn to speak, timelines blurred, blame shifted. I inserted the wrong mothers into the wrong scenes. In my stories, I was three when I was supposed to be four, ten when I was supposed to be two. No matter my age, I was always innocent.

According to our communications group leader, Mother's Day was our big chance to show gratitude. I wrote you a pink slip.

*Thank you for your services.*

The bonding thing wasn't happening for us so I was sent to boarding school—packed up and FedEx-ed. When I came home for the holidays, you had turned my bedroom into a scrapbooking workshop. No hard feelings.

I wondered where I would stay when I came home in June. You told me I was going to finishing school for the summer. In the meantime, I could stay in the guest room.

I knew my father would put an end to this. I called him and asked, "Do I really need to be finished?"

And without pause, he said—yes.

# PLAY
# THE DYING
# CARD

An old man sags in a recliner parked on my front lawn. He wears only green boxers pulled high over his beach ball stomach. As he moves, his zigzag bones poke out in strange places.

He waves to my neighbours who scuttle by in the rain. Some stop and ask if he is okay. In response, the old man bends over and splashes his slippers in a puddle. As it gets wet, his empty duffel bag collapses. A lamp beside him flickers to lightning rhythms.

Someone taps on my backdoor. My neighbour, Edna, holds the skeleton of an umbrella over her head. "There's an old man sitting in a chair in your front yard. I think he's waiting to get inside," she whispers.

"Should I let him in?" I play with the thimbles in my pockets. Tiny bits of armour.

"He looks pretty harmless."

My neighbour has two large Himalayans that press their furry faces against her window all day. I believe she has excellent judgment. I return to my front door and open it. The man cannot raise his head so he looks at me sideways.

"Sergeant Ted, reporting for duty," he says and salutes.

I close the door on him. I, too, once thought he was harmless.


My mother and Sergeant Ted met at *Wash and Tumble Laundry: Home of the Missing Sock*. I liked it there since mother often let me spin in the washers instead of taking a bath. While I was jumping in and out, their underwear got mixed together. Sergeant Ted had sewn address tags into all of his clothes, so mother was able to track him down and reunite him with his green boxers.

"It's the right thing to do," she said as if she were about to spoon-feed a starving nation. When we got there, she pulled into the driveway and told me to wait. She didn't put the underwear in a bag. She handed them over in a big bunch and a few pairs fell on the ground. I don't know why that embarrassed me but I was glad she had left me in the car.

Sergeant Ted stood at the door and accepted the boxers casually, as if he were taking a basket of tomatoes from a neighbour. This was the first time I saw his daughter, Kate. She was around my age, peering out from behind her father's legs. She had blonde pageant curls and wore a large Miss Alaska sash, although we lived nowhere near that state. When my mother and Sergeant Ted were finished talking, she saluted him and tiny wings sprouted from her ankle bones. I wondered what Kate might think of my mother as she stood there in her bare feet, see-through cotton dress and angel wings.

When my mother got back in the car, she was excited she had a date with the Sergeant. "He owns a TV," she said. "And he has a daughter who I think you'll really like."

I thought she had met her prince.


On my front lawn, Edna holds the remains of her umbrella over Sergeant Ted's head while he pulls the light cord. The clouds grow darker and more faceless neighbours appear and huddle on the sidewalk.

When I go outside, I keep my hands in my pockets, thimbles on my fingertips. My feet sink into the water and grass. Mud presses between my toes, tries to cover my feet and hold me down. Each step forward is a deliberate sloshing. It is an act. "Why did you come here?"

"There's something I want to ask you," he says.

"So ask."

"Do you remember where your mother buried her hair?"

The puddles around him form tidal waves and crash at his kneecaps. Lightning threatens in the distance. He strokes the splintered arms of his chair.

"You're not welcome here." I walk away and think of other people's family reunions—planned affairs with invitations and potato salad with too much paprika.

"Wait. I also have something to tell you," Sergeant Ted says.

"So tell."


I cried at my mom and Sergeant Ted's wedding from beginning to end. A flood so great it washed down the aisle and out the door. Everyone rowed or swam to the reception. My mother's dinghy almost tipped over. I lost my paddles.

I blamed myself for their union. At *Wash and Tumble*, I wanted so desperately to touch men's underwear. I had never seen it up close before and was convinced it was something terribly important I was missing out on. So when I saw it, I grabbed it and took it swimming with me. If I had just left it alone, we wouldn't have moved out of our house and I wouldn't have watched my mother wobble in high heels, stuffed into someone else's dress, her hair combed and twisted.


Sergeant Ted watches the water stream down his legs. When he bends over, he looks unhinged at the waist.

Edna says, "My cats get despondent when I'm gone for too long."

"Yes, I understand." I see the cats in the window looking despondent.

"Can we bring this man inside?" she asks.

I click my thimbles together. "He should go."

Edna looks up and down the street. "Where?" She leans in closer. "I think he's trying to tell you something. I think he's dying."

Sergeant Ted does his best to sit straight. "Attention," he says. "Prepare to advance."

He waves my neighbours off the sidewalk. They move forward and hoist Sergeant Ted and his chair into the air.

"Charge!" Sergeant Ted says.

They take a moment to steady themselves, one neighbour positioned under each leg, and then they advance toward the house.

"I won't block your view for long," Sergeant Ted says as he glides by. He asks to be set down gently in front of the TV.

"You can't stay here."

"Thank you for letting me stay here." He settles back into his chair. "Can you please get guest soaps and towels ready? I'd like to take a bath."


My stepsister Kate was an army brat who, by age eleven, had lived in Germany, France and Switzerland. Shortly after the underwear incident, when we were introduced, I thought she already looked tired with life. She was a chameleon, used to fitting in quickly. She could change colours in a blink: red, blue, yellow, orange, silver.

After the wedding, we moved into their army housing.

"Do you like this place?" Kate asked.

I shook my head. I had walked up to six others before I found the door that accepted my key. "They're all beige."

"Same-same. It's so everyone learns to conform," Kate said. While she waited for me to reply, she changed colours. Green, purple, pink, mauve.

"My old house was fuchsia and had magic stained-glass windows."

"What was magic about them?" Her skin paused on fuchsia.

"In the parts that were broken, you could see into another world."

"This house doesn't come with that feature but it sounds cool."

"It was. It was a different world altogether. Not this one."

146

"Well, if you hate this house, we won't be here long." Then she crawled under her bed and came back out with a small tray. It was packed with lipstick and other make-up. "Here," she said and handed me a tube of *Fuchsia Fix.* "Just don't let Sergeant Ted find it or see you with it on."

"He's not the boss of me," I said.

"He's the boss of everyone." Then she told me in Switzerland, she lived in a cuckoo clock; in Germany, she lived in a beer stein; in France, she lived in a hollowed out baguette.

*There were strange noises in that house. At night gurgling pipes sounded like someone being strangled; the roar of the furnace, a tiger thrown into the fire; the clicking of the fridge motor, someone tapping at the door.*

I sit behind Sergeant Ted on the couch. He leaks and oozes all over my floor. He reaches for things that are not there. "Help me find my glasses," he says while he extends his hands. His fingers grapple with the air. Then he fixes imaginary frames around his ears. "These pinch my face but they're better than nothing." He settles in to watch TV, backchats the news, tells me stories about his youth that crumble and turn to dust. "We rode our horses backwards to school, sideways both ways."

"You said you came here to tell me something," I say.

"Did you hear the one about the priest and the rabbi?"

"Attention."

Sergeant Ted came into our room for an inspection. Flames licked the edges of his nostrils with each breath. Kate stood very still beside her bed while he went through her drawers. They were lined with white paper and were filled with perfectly folded clothes and balled up matching socks. He inspected her shelves—items organized by descending height. He took out his ruler and measured the space between her headboard and pillow, between her pillow and the folded blanket.

"Have you been brushing your teeth?" he yelled.

"Affirmative, Sir," Kate yelled back. He poked around in her mouth with a spanner wrench and flashlight.

Mother and I had been studying the house rules posted on the fridge but thought they were jokes written with the kind of humour we didn't understand. At our old house, we had rules on our fridge too: *Be Nice or Leave.*

We knew there would be rules. Mother said a military life would give us structure. No one would knock on the door asking for rent. No more floors unswept or beds unmade.

When Sergeant Ted finished with Kate, he said to me, "One free pass. Next week there will be an inspection."

When he left, Kate sat down on her bed. Pink, red, black, blue. "It's not so bad. I like to just get it over with."

*The last lights in the house go off. Click, click.*

I grab my binoculars and move to Sergeant Ted's side. He stares blankly at the TV. There are liver spots on his face. I connect the dots: Orion's belt, the Little Dipper, Draco. Through her window, Edna is looking at me through her binoculars. She grabs one of her cats and waves its paw. I close the blind. Sergeant Ted looks at me. "What are you doing?" he asks.

"Mapping out constellations." I look at his mouth through my binoculars. "Is there something you'd like to tell me?"

"Why did you let me in?"

"That's asking, not telling."

"Well?"

"My neighbours let you in because you played the dying card."

He clucks his tongue. "Hair still grows even after you die."

I turn the focus dial until everything blurs.

I went into the kitchen and found my mother holding her hair. It had been gathered in an elastic band and chopped off. The ends were jagged, like something had gnawed at it. She swished it around like a horse's tail.

Though she still had wings, she often folded them flat against her legs and kept them tucked inside her socks.

"We could go back to our old house," I whispered. "I know how to get back in through the window." I knew it was still empty because I rode my bike by it every day.

She brushed the tail across my face. "Too late my sweet."

"He does room inspections," I told her. "Do I have to be neat?"

She nodded. A few feathers came loose and floated between us.

"I think we've made a mistake," I whispered.

"This can't be undone." Sergeant Ted had rules for her, too.

"TV isn't so great," I said.

More feathers floated between us and fell to the ground. She swept them up.

*The hallway floorboards have something to say.*

Sergeant Ted shakes as he gets out of his chair. The leather sticks to his legs and fights to hang on to his pale, loose skin. "I'd like to change into my uniform, please."

"So change."

When he shuffles out of the bathroom, he is wearing a billowy faded uniform, a leather pudding-bowl helmet and goggles. He sits down, lights his pipe. Then he spreads his arms and legs and straddles an imaginary motorcycle. "Vroom," he says and twists the throttle.

"You came here to tell me something," I remind him.

"Did I ever tell you about the time I spent in Germany?" He closes his eyes. "I hit a landmine and flew ass over teakettle into the ditch. They couldn't find me for two days."

"Those must have been two very good days."

He revs the engine again and smokes his pipe. "When they finally found me, my laces were still tied up. My boots were still on my feet but my soles were missing."

I listen to his raspy laughter, to the gurgle of old tar in his esophagus. He closes his eyes again and finds the same bombs exploding beneath him, stealing bits of memory and his soles.

My mother said she was going out to bury her hair. It was bad luck to just throw it away. "We don't need any more bad luck, do we?"

"No," I said. Sergeant Ted was bad enough.

"Do you need anything from the store?" she asked.

"I guess I'll need matching socks and a new toothbrush."

"Bring me your old one so I'll know what kind to get."

I went to get my toothbrush, a frayed thing with a worn out Mickey Mouse on the handle. When I came back, she was already gone.

*Shadows slip underneath the door.*

Sergeant Ted is tired after his motorcycle ride around Germany. He settles back down in his chair. "I've only lost my two front teeth. The rest are mine," he tells me and gives a big smile.

I grab one of my dress forms and start to sew on a zipper. I'm making a spacesuit for one of my clients. I can't be distracted by Sergeant Ted's tartar-free gums, his crooked but otherwise healthy incisors. I've got work to do. Deadlines to meet. My client is heading to the moon any day now.

Sergeant Ted sleeps, mouth gaping open. I grab my flashlight, move closer and take a look inside. I see letters hiding behind rotten molars, tucked underneath silver fillings, buried by the weight of his tongue. I take my tweezers and extract the letters one by one. I hold them in my palm and try to arrange them. These are foreign words, if they are words at all.

Sergeant Ted wakes with a snort. "You're sitting very close," he says.

"I wanted to see you."

He covers his eyes with both hands then takes them away and says, "Peek-a-boo, I see you too."

I wash my hands and watch a, b and c swirl down the drain.

When it rained feathers, I knew my mother died on the way to bury her hair. Sergeant Ted picked up a few feathers and said, "Who kills chickens in the city?"

When I told him what happened, he looked at Kate and me and said, "What am I supposed to feed you two?"

At her funeral, my mother sat beside me. "Shouldn't you be up there?" I moved my head in the direction of the coffin.

"Not just yet."

"This might be fun." I thought of all the ways my invisible mother could help me. When the service was over, I got up to leave but I didn't know she wasn't behind me. Sergeant Ted's fingers were a handcuff around my wrist. He pulled me out into the cold. I stared at the open car door, then the long sidewalk. I looked at Kate, already inside, turning blue. "There are fewer shadows when you're around," she said.

She held out her shaking hand, icicles forming on her fingertips. I reached out and tried to warm them.

*Hand on the doorknob. Turn, then release. Turn, then release.*

"Invite these people to my funeral," Sergeant Ted says. He shakes a small address book at me. When I look inside, most of the names, written in pencil, have been erased. The book is filled with the edges of torn out pages, smudges where names used to be.

Kate and I made a confession booth out of a cardboard refrigerator box and an old shower curtain. We used edible candy necklaces for rosaries. We turned off the lights because we thought it would be easier to confess.

"Bless me father for I have sinned," Kate said.

"How long since your last confession, my child?"

"I've never confessed. I have quite a list." I could hear her munching her rosary.

"Where would you like to start?"

"My mother died giving birth to me."

"Why is that something you want to confess?"

"I feel guilty."

"It was not your fault. Child, you are forgiven. Which part of the rosary is your favourite?"

"Watermelon. I'm going to save the rest of my list for later," she said and pulled the shower curtain aside. We switched places.

"Bless me father for I have sinned."

"What did you do?"

"I touched your father's underwear."

"Me, too," she said. "That's also on my list." I parted the shower curtain to see her stroke it off her paper. Her skin turned blue and stayed that way for a long time.

*Wait. Wait. Wait.*

Sergeant Ted's chair creaks as he leans over to strike a match on its wood frame. He is dying of lung cancer but at seventy-five insists, "It's been bloody long enough."

"I agree."

He taps his pipe. He starts every one with three puffs then smokes until my living room is filled with a fog neither of us can find our way through. "Do you know where Kate is?" he asks.

"No, do you want me to try and find her?" I've heard being surrounded by family can help a person die faster.

He nods, then falls asleep. His pipe spills. I watch a large ash smoulder on the chair, burning itself out.

To solve the meal problem, Sergeant Ted gave Kate and me army ration packs for our school lunches. "Just add water," he said.

We sold the dehydrated flakes to boys who found the gelatinous substance very useful. We used the money to buy food and make-up. In our beige world, a blossoming collection seemed very important. We bought lipstick in shades of *Sassy Spice*, *Wow Violet* and *Surge Butter*. We bought blush in shades of *Smouldering Wine* and *Iced Lotus*.

In the morning, after Sergeant Ted left for work, we would apply liberally and repeat as necessary. I narrowed her wide nose. She widened my narrow-set eyes. We contoured each other's inadequate cheekbones. We did everything we could to blend, blend, blend. At school, we spent six hours thoroughly and blissfully trolloped. Then we would race home and slip back into our blotchy, oily skin.

*The dark cloud passes over my bed.*

Though years pass between our conversations, Kate picks up exactly where we left off.

"I told the drycleaner my suit is now two different colours. But he never did give me a refund. Anyway, how are you?"

She is one of those people who like to seem busier than they really are so little effort is required on my part. "Sergeant Ted is dying. He'd like to see you."

"It's good to want things," she says.

Throughout our conversation, she punctuates pauses so it will seem like her words must first sail across an ocean to reach me.

"I'm not coming," she says. She is also the type of person who thinks her decisions mean more when they hurt people.

"You're coming for me," I say.

When I get off the phone, I poke Sergeant Ted awake. I love the startled grunt he makes. The way his feet find their place on the ground. The way he looks around for snipers then sees a *Price Is Right* rerun, Bob Barker on TV reminding him to spay or neuter his pet.

"Kate is on her way."

"I'll stay alive until she gets here," he says.

"While we're waiting, is there something you'd like to tell me?" I watch the three white hairs on the top of his head wave back and forth.

"I don't suppose you remember..."

"Go on."

"Where our dog Abe was buried?"

I pluck the three hairs from his head and surrender too easily, because it's all I can do.

The boys at school started wanting more than Kate's rations. One made the mistake of showing up at our house. He asked Sergeant Ted, casually, if she was allowed to hang out with him.

"Not tonight," said Sergeant Ted, and we waited for the door to slam, for the earth to shake, for him to come into our room and breathe fire. Instead, he went back to the kitchen and we heard him rummaging through the fridge.

Before we went to bed, he said, "I don't want you two walking home by yourselves tomorrow. There's a pervert on the loose."

After our last class, we wiped off our make-up in the school bathroom. We walked outside and saw an army tank parked on the lawn. Sergeant Ted popped the lid and gave a parade wave to the gathering crowd. The boy from the night before crawled out charred and shredded. Kate walked forward, turned a brilliant shade of *Just Pinched* and sank into the pit. I stood paralyzed as Sergeant Ted climbed out, lifted me up and carried me on my side like a plank. Kate's relationship with boys returned strictly to the selling of dehydrated flakes.

*In my old house, you could look through broken stained glass and go anywhere.*

Headlights flash across the living room window. I hear Kate cut the engine. I look through the blinds and see her sitting in a rented convertible, staring straight ahead, hands still locked on the wheel. It is raining. The car is filled with water. A little girl sits beside her wearing a lifejacket and snorkel. There is a light breeze blowing Kate's scarf. She looks like she's still driving. The static from my TV is her soundtrack. From the streetlight glow, her skin looks radiant, cheekbones contoured. Her hair is gathered in a loose knot. I put on my thimbles and wait.

I heard the window slide open in the middle of the night. Felt the smack of cold air. Was someone coming or going? I shook my firefly jar and found Kate's bed empty. There was a silver fingerprint on the glass. In *Crushed Orange* lipstick, she wrote *MIA* over her bed.

I heard Sergeant Ted turn off the last lights. Click. Click. He opened our bedroom door and saw Kate was gone. "Where is she?"

"I don't know." I used my firefly jar to keep him away.

He ripped Kate's drawers out. Balls of socks went flying. Books, tallest to shortest, crashed off the shelves.

He tore the mattress off the bed. I feared *Forever Fuchsia* and *Breathless Berry* would spill across the floor, but they stayed hidden in our secret tray. He went back to the drawers and found a container of *Cherry Blossom* lip gloss hidden in a pair of Kate's underwear. He sniffed it. For a moment the wrinkles ironed themselves off his face. Then he was on top of me, digging into cherry and smearing it across my face.

*The bedsprings moan under the weight of him.*

When Kate releases the wheel, I close my eyes and listen to the sound of rushing water, then the clip-clop of high heels on pavement. Kate doesn't knock. She walks through the door, clicks her briefcase on the floor and slides out of her shoes as if she's just returning home from work.

"Hi," I say and hand them towels. The little girl looks at me from behind Kate's legs. Big Kate and Little Kate.

"Hi," Big Kate says. She tries to detach Little Kate from her legs.

"Hello." I wave to Little Kate.

"Hello," she says. "In London, we live inside Big Ben and I go to school on The Tube."

"That sounds like fun." Pointing to Big Kate's ridiculous crocodile bag, I say, "I like that."

"Cranberry red. Wasn't that your favourite?"

"Fuchsia."

"Ah, yes. I remember." She looks around. "It's creepy in here with all of the mannequins."

"They're dress forms. Only a few are mannequins."

Kate looks at her father. "Did I make it?"

"Did I make it?" Little Kate imitates while talking through her snorkel.

"She does that when she's nervous," Big Kate says, swatting at the girl.

"She does that when she's nervous," Little Kate repeats. She starts doing the breaststroke around my living room.

I climbed out the window and followed her silver footprints until they disappeared. When they stopped, I stopped. I stood there and knew she would never leave me. Without her, he only had me.

I waited years for her return.

"Well?" Kate says, waving her phone. "Did I make it?"

"Well? Did I make it?" Little Kate says.

Big Kate puts her hand over Little Kate's mouth. Little Kate tries to bite her mother's fingers. Big Kate lets go.

"You can't control them," Big Kate says. She walks over to Sergeant Ted. She grabs the remote from his hand and turns off the TV. She reaches out to touch his head but hovers over it instead. Then she pulls away, as if she's been stung.

Little Kate walks over and stares. Sergeant Ted's pipe dangles from his mouth like an upside down comma—a sentence left unfinished. A string of saliva pulls from his lips as Big Kate takes the pipe and lights it for herself. "Thank god I was on business in New York and not London or it would have taken me forever to get here."

"Yes, that was convenient," I say.

Sergeant Ted startles awake. Little Kate stands in front of him. "Are you going to die while I'm standing right here watching?"

"I hope not," Sergeant Ted says.

Big Kate blows smoke in his face. He coughs and turns toward her. "Hello, Katie."

She hands back his pipe. "Keep smoking."

"Keep smoking!" Little Kate says.

"Did I ever tell you about the time I spent in Germany?" he asks Little Kate.

"Nope." Little Kate pulls up a chair.

Sergeant Ted is tired but manages to spin tales in which he is always the hero, in which he stands in harm's way to protect others. He saves little girls from burning castles. He helps lost people find their way home. There are explosions, which, he admits, have altered his memory somewhat. He keeps talking and talking. His breathing gets shallower and more forced.

Big Kate takes his pipe and smokes until a cloud forms over his head. Finally, just outside Düsseldorf, a bomb takes him out.

"This old guy's sleepy," Little Kate says.

Big Kate turns the colour of joy. When the paramedics arrive, she says, "Do not resuscitate."

They pack him up and the chair sits empty. Sergeant Ted once told me it had an eject mechanism and if I dared to sit in it, it would send me to the moon. I pull on my client's spacesuit and get Little Kate to zip it up. I slowly lower myself into the chair. I feel the frame and springs press into my bones, dig into my skin. The leather is worn. I close my eyes, grip the armrests and have never felt farther from the moon.

Little Kate looks around at the dress forms. "Are you my aunt?" she asks.

"Are you my aunt?" I ask her back.

"No." She starts laughing.

I see the appeal of her game but Big Kate turns *Volcanic Red*. "I guess I'm your aunt. Sort of."

"Auntie Sort-Of, can you make me a ball gown? Apparently, I'm going to a funeral."

"Sergeant Ted wishes to be buried sitting in his chair," the lawyer reads.

The funeral director doesn't think a chair coffin is a good idea. Then he works out the price and says, "I'd be happy to accommodate your father's most unusual final request."

"Stepfather," I correct as he hands me the estimate.

"He must have been quite a character," he says.

"Yes, quite a character," Big Kate says.

"Yes, quite a character," Little Kate says.

"Don't take your death lying down," Big Kate says as we're leaving. She looks at me and says, "That's British humour."

"That's why it's not funny," Little Kate tells me.


The red taffeta for Little Kate's dress comes down the chimney, slips underneath the door, pours out the taps, fills up my tub, overflows my kitchen sink. Little Kate stands on a chair, eyes closed, arms held out at her sides. She doesn't wiggle when the cold tape measure goes around her.

"Is there enough fabric for a train, Auntie Sort-Of?"

"I think so."

Big Kate floats on a life raft in the red sea and tells us how dresses are made in Italy. She stresses the importance of boning, says it gives structure but can make it difficult to breathe. She paddles over to dry land and offers to help. She grabs the material underneath Little Kate's armpit and gouges her while pinning the fabric together. Little Kate grabs my pinking shears and makes crinkled threats.

"Testy, testy," Big Kate says. She puts the pins down and holds her hands in the air. Then she grabs a mannequin and starts to dance. I help Little Kate down and find her a small partner. I grab my own mannequin. We are all on dry land dancing fearlessly with our neutered men.


Little Kate, in her red ball gown, walks up to Sergeant Ted—hands on her hips. Big Kate and I sit in the first row and stare at his open coffin. It looks like an outhouse made of lacquered mahogany. He sits upright in his chair, hands folded on his lap.

"The funeral director said he'll have to be buried deeper than six feet," I tell Big Kate.

"How deep?"

"At least twelve feet."

"That's a good depth."

When Little Kate is finished inspecting Sergeant Ted, she stands back and twirls around and around. She holds her dress up, showing flashes of white underwear.

Big Kate gets up. I grab her icy blue hand and we walk toward him. I poke Sergeant Ted's face. His skin is firm but supple. The dent I made doesn't fill in so I make a few more. He is a wax doll wearing make-up. *Tiptoe through the Tulips* on his cheeks, *Tomato Yum* on his lips.

Big Kate pinches the sides of his mouth, revealing the wires that are keeping it shut.

"I'm sorry," he says, with deep remorse.

"You came all this way to tell me that?" I say. "You shouldn't have."

Formaldehyde dribbles down his chin. I unfold his rubbery hands and jam my thimbles onto his fingertips. Then I grab one of Little Kate's hands and Big Kate grabs the other. Together, we stop the little girl from spinning.

# ACKNOWLEDGEMENTS

My sincere thanks to the editors of magazines in which these stories first appeared in various forms: Nick Mount (*The Walrus*, "Airplanes Couldn't be Happier in Turbulence" and "Somewhere, a Long, Happy Life Probably Awaits You"); Gerard Beirne (*The Fiddlehead*, "The Problem with Babies" and "A Box Full of Wildebeest"); Kim Jernigan (*The New Quarterly*, "Play the Dying Card"); and Mark Anthony Jarman (*Coming Attractions*, Oberon Press).

For their mentorship and generosity, I am grateful to Charlotte Gill and Lisa Moore.

I've had some lovely writerly friends along the way; in particular, Armin Wiebe, Rosemary Nixon, Shawn Stibbards, Pam Chamberlain, John Mooney and my editors Josina Robb and John K. Samson.

I've long been an admirer of artist Julie Morstad's work and am happy to make my debut with her lovely *Playhouse* along for the ride.

Finally, if you've journeyed through this book from start to finish, I am grateful for you, my readers.